Tales & Typos

By J. E. Tankersley

First Edition

Cover design and illustrations by Bodie H.

Edited by Katie Lasitter

ISBN 979-8-9855546-0-1 (PB)

ISBN 979-8-9855546-1-8 (EB)

For Finn.
Wait, you're a baby. You can't even read.
For Brooke, then.

Tales & Typos

CONTENTS

FOREWORD

For little adventurers, the lines between what's real and what's imagined aren't so very clear. The two have a bad habit of overlapping, blending together until the edges are fuzzy and you can't tell where the real stuff ends, and the make-believe begins.

It's not always on purpose, either. Kids don't plan for adventure to sweep them away to some faraway land. They don't plot out their characters or talk about motivations. They just round the corner into an ordinary bedroom—the kind with off-white walls and more than a few hand-me-down toys—and ask each other a simple question:

"What do you want to play?"

That's all it takes.

The next moment, they're winding their way up a narrow staircase by torchlight, shushing one another a little too loudly, watching as their shadows stretch across the dark stone walls. They creep up each cold step, keeping their eyes peeled for danger, ready to pounce at the first sign of trouble. After all, it's not every day you find yourself exploring the spindly towers protruding from a castle in the sky, and there's no telling what you might find next.

"A giant used to live here, you know?" One might say to another, narrowing their eyes into paper-thin slits to peer deeper into the darkness. "They say he used to walk around out there—out on the clouds—and *that's* where thunder comes from."

"Everybody knows *that*," another might snort, knowing full and well they'd never heard such a thing before. "But there's nothing to be scared of. This place has been abandoned for centuries—which is like a *million* years."

"Abandoned? That's not what *I* heard," a third could reply. "*I* heard that, at the top of this tower, something's waiting. Something big. Something *evil*. I heard there's—"

A dragon, of course. With fire and wind and darkness it would appear, and their little hearts would alight with the thrill and terror of it all. In a flurry of screams and roars (which to the untrained ear can sound an awful lot like being mauled by an actual dragon), the little heroes would set iron against the worm's diamond scales. They'd dip and dive, roll and crawl, desperate to avoid the legendary flames that vaporize water and turn flesh to ash with a single touch.

Adventures are so often like that. They happen in the blink of an eye. Pillows become shields. Broom handles become blades. Feathers become flames.

But not once during these quests do you ever see a child stop, hold up their hands, and shout, "Alright, now hold on! Just stop. This isn't a cloud castle at all. This is your mom's bedroom. We're in your house, and that's not a staff. It's just a cardboard tube. None of this is real!"

Because to them, it *is* real. Or, at the very least, it's as real as anything can ever hope to be.

Imagination is a special thing. It's a mystical, magical, wonderful thing that can at once teleport us to unknown worlds or send us careening into the dripping jaws of danger. It gives us the opportunity to explore strange places, meet fantastical people, and have the kinds of adventures that are, in my experience, sorely lacking in the *real* real world. And the best part is, imagination is utterly, entirely, and irrevocably free. It grants us our every wish and asks for only one thing in return—that we believe.

And that's really where the trouble begins. As we get older, we often find that believing isn't as easy as it once was, and by the time most of us reach our third decade, we've altogether forgotten that magical power we once wielded as children.

We forget that a towel can become a cloak of invisibility, that aluminum foil is a wonderful substitute for plate mail, that the wind from a ceiling fan can gust like a hurricane. We forget about the sea of clouds churning beneath the railing of our back porch, that there's a cavern full of monsters in the attic, that the floor is lava. And even though most of us never realize it, we're desperate to remember.

Maybe that's why so many of us are ravenous readers. Maybe that's why we're willing to pay forty dollars to spend two hours in a movie theater, or why we're content to binge our favorite shows for the third time. Maybe that's why I spend my weekends around a tabletop, playing games, and telling stories, and doing elementary school math with other adults. Because it helps me remember.

For those of you who don't know, tabletop role-playing games can best be described as a kind of collaborative storytelling where friends get together, roll some dice, and play pretend. At the table, we all agree to be someone else for a spell, to exit our bodies for a few hours as we dive headlong into a story. And, perhaps most importantly, we all agree to make memories together—the real kind.

Make-believe comes naturally to children. After all, they've yet to forget how magical imagination truly is. But for those of us cursed with the condition called *adulthood*, time around the tabletop is precious.

There are no taxes or chores when you're playing pretend. There are no bills on the counter or reports to file. There are no grocery lists, or oil changes, or lawns to mow. With dice in hand, there are no Mondays. There is only the call to adventure.

The memories we make around the table are special. Few of us can even recall the room where we made them. We don't remember the sound of dice clacking, or the shuffling of papers, or the scent of warm beer that tends to permeate the space after a few hours of dungeon delving. Instead, we remember our adventures the way that children do—as if they really happened. As if we were there.

We recall our skin puckering at the chill of the crypt. We remember the thrumming of our hearts as we crept into the dragon's lair. In our minds, we can still smell the dust of the dungeon floor, see the flash of our blades, and hear the melodious chant of our incantations.

When we see a character fall, we feel the loss as if we'd watched them take that final gulp of air with our own eyes. Some might argue, "Those people weren't real. It's all fiction. You can't mourn the loss of someone who never existed." But we know better.

Like most memories, we rarely reflect on the stories in their entirety. They come to us in flashes and scenes and moments—little windows of time where the most important details still call out to us.

There are times when we cling to the beginnings or the ends, and other times where we favor those bits in the middle. We might recall how the druid saved us all with a clever spell that bound our enemies up tight in thorns and thistle, yet the moments just before and after might be lost to us altogether. In any case, all the little particulars eventually grow blurry and distant with time, as most good memories tend to do.

Tales & Typos is a collection of stories inspired by memories and make-believe. Some are true retellings of moments from around my living room coffee table, while others were simply inspired by the people I've met, the places I've been, and the magical things I've seen while playing pretend.

For those who've never rolled dice and spoken in a funny accent around a tabletop, I hope these stories remind you of your favorite childhood adventures, when your imagination was endless, and your understanding of plot holes was limited. If nothing else, I hope they're able to take you away for a bit—to meet someone you haven't yet met, to go somewhere new.

But for those of you who know the sound of dice against wood, the rush of a natural twenty, or the crushing weight of its opposite, I hope these tales help you recall stories from time spent around your own table. I hope they remind you of what makes those memories so special, and I hope they inspire you to go make more.

More than anything, I hope these stories will make you want to ask the question, "What do you want to play?"

After all, there are a great many wonders to be found while adventuring, whether in this world or the many, many others we sometimes find ourselves roaming.

I t was mid-autumn when Chamomile Tenpenny found herself northward bound on the well-trodden footpath between the Elderwild and the picturesque town of Bramblebrush.

Now, this wasn't one of those rainy, soggy sorts of fall days that so often appear in the latter half of the season. It was a perfect day—all golden light and crisp air and blue sky. It was the kind of day where the sun beams brightly from above, where only a smattering of wisp-like clouds dares to gather on the border of the horizon, afraid to spoil the view.

Chamomile, as unfortunate as some might believe it to be, hadn't taken notice of these lovely details. In fact, as she bobbed along the trail with her texts and scrolls and mace rattling with each step, her hazel eyes remained firmly affixed to the ground.

She couldn't be bothered to notice how the leaves fell gently against the wind, whipping here and there in playful tufts of red and orange, begging her to chase them about in the chill. She didn't notice the faint smell of a campfire wafting through the air or the crunch of brown things beneath her feet. She wasn't at all aware of the way her auburn curls held the view beyond her freckled face like a fall-themed picture frame. She simply walked, as if her mind was somewhere else and her body had places to be.

Typically, on a day like today, Chamomile would be all too eager to seek out a half-shaded, moss-ridden tree to post up beneath. You know, the kind where the roots and vines at the bottom form a sort of daybed around their guest, gently cradling them and keeping the sun out of their eyes. Father Appletop used to say they were the perfect place to pour over a verse of scripture or two (or in Chamomile's experience, the ideal setting for an afternoon nap).

Sadly, today was not an ordinary day, and this usually cheery halfling was walking with a not-so-ordinary sense of urgency. She had spent too long in Ramshorn, and both her coin purse and her belly were all too aware of it. One was protesting loudly beneath her chain shirt while the other pouted silently against her hip.

"No, *of course,* sister! I will stay for as long as you need, *sister,*" she groaned, drawing out the words in a stage-worthy fashion. "Payment? *Payment?* I wouldn't *dream* of such a thing. I'm here to help, after all. Stale bread, you say? My *favorite.*"

Chamomile walked a little faster. She pinched the bridge of her nose and rubbed her eyes.

"Stupid girl. Now what are you going to do?"

For the better part of two weeks, Chamomile had been working at the church in Ramshorn. Two weeks too many, if you asked her. For fourteen hours each day, she traveled from cot to cot, providing healing to the sick, reciting prayers, mopping up blood with dirty rags, changing bedpans, that sort of thing. But what did she have to show for it?

Her stomach answered the rhetorical question.

"I know, I know," she moaned, placing a sympathetic hand against her belly. "No need to get nasty about it. Who taught you that kind of language, anyway? I'll find you something to eat in Bramblebrush. Promise."

"I don't mean to pry," a tired, tinny voice said. "But who are you talking to?"

Chamomile nearly jumped out of her skin. As if jolted awake by a charging beast, one hand flew for her mace, and the other shot up in a defensive stance.

On the side of the path, sitting cross-legged atop an old tree stump, was a hunched man holding a walking stick. He had a frizzy beard the color of dove's feathers, and the folds of skin around his eyes were deep and purple. His robes were frayed and patched in places, and the bottoms of his shoes were nearly worn through. Chamomile could see a single pinky toe peeping out from beneath the paper-thin leather.

He blinked a few times beneath a set of wiry eyebrows, patiently awaiting a response. She had been so wrapped up in her one-sided conversation that she might have walked right past him had he not spoken.

With wide eyes and a half-raised mace, Chamomile felt her face go flush.

"I'm so sorry!" She said, a little too loudly, and an embarrassed laugh came after. She released her weapon and fumbled with where to put her hands. "I didn't see you there. My stomach was protesting the service in this establishment, and I—well, sorry."

The man gave a knowing nod.

"Ah. I find that bellies are often the toughest negotiators."

Chamomile forced a grin and scratched the back of her head. She was mortified, but the stranger's kind expression softened the blow. To think, she'd nearly knocked the white from his beard. How would she have explained that to the church?

"Well, don't mind me, then. Good day to you!"

She gave a single stilted nod and scooted a bit down the path.

"If I could trouble you," he said, raising a wrinkled and knotted hand toward her. "It seems our stomachs have much in common. Could I be so bold as to ask for a coin? Just enough for a small meal this evening. I was just on my way to Ramshorn, you see, but it seems I've lost my purse somewhere along the way."

There was something disarming about his tone, and—though he didn't know it—she *had* almost smashed his face in a moment ago. A single coin was a small price to pay for a clear conscience.

"Of course, no problem at—"

Chamomile's breath hitched as her fingertips reached the bottom of her coin purse. Beside a ball of lint and an old hairpin, there was a single silver piece. She traced its cool edge, remembering that her time in town had been unpaid. It was all she had left.

She stared at the old man for a beat. If she gave him this, there would be no warm stew at the end of the night, no bath at the inn to soak her aching muscles, and no bed to curl up in after. She would have nothing, and her night would be spent sleeping beneath a musty blanket on the cold ground outside of town.

She gazed into his deep wrinkles, the ones that scrunched up atop his smile. She saw his worn-through shoes. His dirty knuckles. His tattered robe.

"Of course," she repeated. "No problem at all."

Chamomile plucked the last remaining coin from her purse and held it out in her palm.

"Just promise to use what's left on a new pair of shoes, huh?" She asked.

The old man stared at the silvery disk in the girl's hand like an adventurer stumbling onto a dragon's mountainous hoard. Slowly, and with trembling hands, he reached out and took it, gripping the coin tightly with all his fingers.

"Thank you." He breathed the words more than he spoke them, placing the coin into a patchwork satchel beside the stump.

"Of course," she said. "Enjoy that meal, and may the Lightmaker shine upon you and all that."

Chamomile then turned to continue down the path, still hungry and dreading the night to come but satisfied all the same. She'd only made it a few steps when the stranger's voice called out once again.

"Before you go," he said, rising from the stump, "I'd like to repay you somehow. I have no silver or gold, you know, but maybe there is something else. A gift, perhaps?"

Chamomile snorted. "It's just a silver piece. It's nothing, really."

"No, no. I insist," he said, dismissing her by flapping a limp hand in her general direction.

His brow furrowed into a mock-serious expression.

"Can't go around building up debts to every little halfling girl around the countryside, now can I?"

She rolled her eyes dramatically and crossed back toward the stump where the stranger was busy rustling through his bag.

"Ah, there we have it," he said. "Now, close your eyes and hold out your hand."

Chamomile did as she was told, and there was a rustling and a jingling from the bag. She held out her hand, anticipating the weight and temperature of the object to come, but nothing happened.

A moment passed, and the little woods grew quiet. The autumn birds chirped in the sun. The leaves shook in the breeze. One of the last bees of the season buzzed around her. But nothing fell into her palm.

She scrunched up her face and called out to the stranger, whose name she didn't know, so she just called him mister. Only the soft hum of the woods responded. Chamomile opened her eyes then, but the old man had vanished. She spun about, calling after him and peering into the trees, but there wasn't a trace of him to be found.

A glimmer of light caught her eye then. There were two objects lying in the center of the tree stump, one that shimmered in the noon-day sun and one that crinkled in the cool breeze. As she approached to inspect them, her heart leapt up to her throat, sticking there like a dry bit of stale bread from the Ramshorn church.

It was a ruby—perfectly cut and nearly the size of her palm, gleaming crimson in the light. Beneath it was a letter, addressed to her by name and written in an elegant, purple script that glittered like stardust.

Chamomile,

Pardon the swift exit, but I really am in quite a rush, you know. It was lovely to meet you, and I should very much like to do so again sometime.

You have proven, as so many of your kind have before you, that if a person's stature were measured by the size of their hearts, halflings might just tower above us all.

The people of this world are lucky to have giants like you among them.

—A

In the distance, Chamomile heard a low, rushing sound, like a pair of enormous wings beating against the autumn air. She shielded her eyes from the light, searching for the source of the whoosh, and right then, for the first time, bathed in the crisp air and glowing sun, she realized how beautiful of a day it had turned out to be after all.

THE HUSH

All was still within Ephraim's Antiques & Artifacts. Shadows stretched like sleepy house cats across the dusty furniture and forgotten keepsakes, and the only sound splitting the silence was the steady tick of an old grandfather clock in the misty display window. It stood there proudly, with its peeling varnish and water-stained base, tick-tick-ticking away, drenched in the pale moonlight. Its decorative hour hand rotated, almost imperceptibly, creeping ever closer to the three. Last call.

Outside, the town of Bramblebrush had tucked in for the night. Windows hung like black bedsheets against the surrounding stucco, *Open* signs were flipped to *Closed*, and the streets were cool and quiet. Here and there, a drunkard could be seen stumbling his way home in the dark, haunted by wisps of fog that strolled along the cobblestones like homesick apparitions. The nearby gutter dripped what remained of the afternoon's rainstorm, a rhythmic plink that kept time with the clock inside.

There was a single lamppost here—a black iron thing with rusty patches and hazy glass. Its oily flame flickered and hissed, pushing against the darkness and illuminating the mismatched stones beneath it, which glistened in the late-night dew. Across the street stood a narrow alleyway, where the lamplight cast a crooked shadow, and it was here within the darkness that a small voice could be heard whispering words of encouragement, not much louder than the ticking of a grandfather clock.

"Just breathe," it said. "You can do this. You can do this."

A beat of silence.

"You *can* do this, right?"

Marigold stood with her back against the wall, staring at the fuzzy outline of her hands in the dim. The new gloves were stiff and tight, and they still squeaked a bit when she made a fist. Her hands felt clammy and clumsy inside them.

The thick black hood that sat ruffled atop her shoulders wasn't much better. It slipped down over her eyes again, and she tugged it back in place with a huff. The tailors of Bramblebrush had little experience crafting garments for young gnomes, and even after the alterations, the cloak swallowed her like a child wearing their parent's winter coat. Nevertheless, Marigold stood there in the dark, waiting, feeling like a kid in a costume.

She counted to ten again, breathing in through her nose and out through her mouth, silently tapping her foot, stamping the jitters away. By now, the clock face across the street was nearly in an L shape. Almost time.

"Of *course* you can do this. It's just a simple lift," she muttered. "In and out. Bing, bang, boom. And that's it. You did it. You passed. You're *in*."

None of the lessons warned her about this part. The racing heart. The trembling knees. The way her stomach kept tightening and relaxing on its own and the waves of nausea that came with it. Where was this in class? She always assumed she would feel confident, and prepared, and, well, cool. In her too-big cloak and squeaky gloves, Marigold did not feel *cool*.

Half a block away, the tavern door swung open with a thwack. The dying laughter inside spilled out onto the flagstones, carrying with it the voices of several men as they stumbled into the night, all red faced and wobbly. The little gnome crept toward the edge of the alleyway and peeped with one eye toward the sound.

She saw three gentlemen staggering her way. The leftmost man was tall and thin with birdish features and an Adam's apple the size of a ripe plum. He wore dirty glasses that sat at the tip of his nose, and his hair was oil slick. That wasn't him. The brief didn't say anything about crane-like legs that walked with all the confidence of a newborn giraffe trying to find its footing.

In the center, there was a middle-aged business type with olive skin and a black tie that dangled beneath a stern, bearded face. He had broad shoulders and a powerful build, and though he was almost certainly drunk himself, he strode with all the poise and sobriety of a teeto-taler. That *definitely* wasn't him. Too tall. Too handsome.

Then on the right side, there was a short, round man sporting a top hat. He looked like a bowling ball drifting toward the gutter, and he walked with his stubby arms stretched out to his sides for balance. He had a thick, curly mustache and beady eyes that struggled to peer over a set of plump and rosy cheeks.

The man in the middle said something unintelligible, and the round man on the right unleashed a whooping, snorting laugh that sounded an awful lot like a piglet splashing in the mud. He gripped his belly with both hands and rocked back and forth, squealing in delight, dabbing at his little eyes with a posh hanky.

That was him.

Then they were walking again, stumbling closer and nearly at the edge of the lamplight. There was no time to think. Marigold adjusted her hood one last time, took a gulp of air, and rounded the corner into the street.

"Eyes on the ground," she thought. "Just ahead of your feet. Hands open. Shoulders slack. Unimposing. Small. Gray."

Her feet slapped quietly against the wet stones as she closed the distance. The round man was still recovering from his cackling fit. With every sigh and giggle, the sound grew closer, closer, closer.

"The moment the bag is in view," she told herself. "One quick motion. Cut and grab. Cut and grab."

The grandfather clock in the display window of Ephraim's Antiques & Artifacts struck three. Marigold stiffened.

And then, it happened.

In the frame of her hood, a bag appeared, jingling softly in the low light. It was a small brown sack with a golden string, loosely clinging to the round man's leather belt, which disappeared beneath the overhang of his belly.

Marigold didn't breathe. She took a half step to the left as she passed the men. One hand shot for the woolen coin purse, and the other silently snipped the rope.

One quick motion.

Everything else was a blur. Sprinting feet. Heavy breathing. The sound of a drunken commotion fading behind her. Marigold darted into an alley, then another, then out into a small side street. She ran as fast as her short legs could carry her—a little black streak cutting through the streetlights before plunging into the shadows again. As she raced into another alleyway, her too-big hood slipped over her eyes again.

Just as the world went black, pain shot through her nose and cheek as it collided—hard—with the knee of a tall man exiting the alley. She crashed to the ground and rolled across the damp street. The taste of blood found its way into her mouth and nose, a sour, metallic flavor. The purse clanged to the cobblestones.

The man knelt down in the darkness and lifted the bag. He tried to apologize as Marigold scrambled back up, then held out the purse toward her. Keeping her face hidden, she snatched her prize, muttered a thank you, and tore off into the shadows once more.

After what felt like an hour, she rounded a corner into a dead-end alleyway somewhere on the other side of town and collapsed to the wet stones, gasping for air. Her legs were shaking again, though this time exhaustion was to blame, not nerves.

It hadn't gone perfectly. She knew that. But she was safe, and she'd done it. She didn't see the man in the alley's face, but he didn't see hers, either. That's all that mattered. Allowing herself to feel proud for a moment, a shallow smile curled the edges of her lips.

It took ages to catch her breath, but when she finally did, Marigold took out the coin purse, untied the golden string, flipped the bag on its head, and emptied the contents on a nearby crate. As the things inside tumbled out in the dark, there was no clang. Rather, it was a clack. Not the clink or clank of gold and copper, but the rattle and clatter of wood and bone.

Marigold stared down at a pile of dice, at least a hundred of them. Little cubes of various sizes, all brown and cream, with dots and numbers from one to six. There was something else, too. A square of paper folded tightly and jutting out from the pile.

She plucked it free and stepped back against the wall, where the moonlight found its way to the stones below. The words inside were written in simple black letters—just like the brief. She read them twice, crumpled the paper into a ball, and ran her tongue along the grooves of her molars, trying not to laugh. It was the oddest mix of frustration and pride, glee and shame.

Thanks for the coin.
Oh, and next time,
try not to look so nervous.
Welcome to The Hush.

Another day, another quest. Elwood plodded along in the damp, crumpling his face into a hundred different expressions, all of which read as indignant, disgruntled, forlorn, hungry, or some combination of the four. There was a nagging feeling in the back of his mind, and despite his many attempts to vanish it by humming songs or fantasizing about dinner, it kept pushing its way to the front.

Adventuring was nothing at all like he imagined as a kid.

More often than not, they spent half their time searching for goblins that didn't exist and the other half explaining to customers that, yes, they do, in fact, still need to pay, even if the goblins weren't real. You'd think folks would be happy their farms weren't overrun with little green monsters, but you'd be mistaken.

So, sure, they were actually getting paid for today's little excursion, but a measly ten silver hardly seemed worth it. The leather straps of Elwood's pack slid down his rain-soaked shoulders again, and he jerked them back into place with a huff.

It's an adventure, Elwood, he told himself. *A man has gone missing, Elwood. This is what heroes do, Elwood.*

The voice in his head sounded like it was reading from a poorly written script, and it was selling the lines with all the believability of an understudy's understudy. Elwood stubbed his toe on another rock, and his internal mono-logue started improvising.

I mean, come on*, man. Couldn't this idiot have gotten lost in a butterfly garden? A nice little beach resort? A brewery? Why did it have to be all the way out* here*?*

The five-mile hike up the mountain would've been miserable under any circumstances. The first half was nothing but jagged rocks and roots that seamed hellbent on twisting Elwood's ankles, and the second half was all sheer cliff faces and, for that little extra razzle dazzle, the ever-present threat of death via rockslide. The incessant downpour that seemed to follow them from town felt like overkill.

Elwood's boots were soaked through, his lunch had been stolen by a particularly deft goat halfway up the mountain, and an endless sheet of water was sliding down his hair and dripping into his ears. That's just what he needed—an ear infection.

Was this really what passed for adventure these days? Where were the battles? The danger? The blood-pumping moments of courage and audacity? Elwood had a hard time imagining that this was what the heroes in all those stories dealt with between the good parts. He certainly never read any tales about a hero slogging up the side of a mountain, wondering how they were going to afford another trip to the apothecary. A third of ten silver certainly wasn't going to cut it.

By the time he and his two companions found them-selves hunched down, crawling through some slimy, rotten cave—which reeked to high hell, by the way—Elwood was over it. He was convinced that this was, in fact, not an adventure. It was a job. Not even a career. Just a job—one with low pay and a non-existent benefits package.

"You should unclench your jaw, Elwood," Marissa suggested without turning back to look at him.

The elf's soft voice bounced off the cavern walls, nagging him from all sides. Elwood glared at the back of her head as she carefully slipped beneath another low-hanging stalactite.

"I think we're close."

She glanced back toward the others then, and the torchlight glinted in her eyes. It was a look that said, "Be ready."

Elwood huffed and took the bow off his back. Be ready for what, a dead end? To bump his head again? He felt silly for even bringing a weapon. Bows were for adventures. This was a hike. He should've brought jerky and an apple, or maybe a good book to read.

"What makes you think we're close?" Grizmo asked.

The little tinkerer rattling along between Elwood and Marissa was working hard to balance the overflowing pack on his shoulders. He shimmied his hips and adjusted his tool belt again, then leaned to one side to keep the top of his bag from catching on the stalactite.

Marissa tapped the tip of her nose.

"Client said the guy was hunting mushrooms, right? I can smell them," she said.

Elwood wasn't sure how she could smell much of anything down here. His nose was full of nothing but wet stone and stale, moldy air. As he stretched over a jagged crack in the floor, Elwood placed his hand on the wall for balance. His fingers pressed into something thick and sticky, and as he yanked it away, the gooey substance came with it in long, silvery strands.

Elwood's eye twitched. Adventuring sucked. The first thing he was doing when they got back to town was putting in an application to the baker. Less work, better pay, and free bread ends. Plus, he was pretty sure he over-heard Lucille at the tavern talking about how Mr. Greyson offered paid time off. His hands could be covered in flour right now.

The descent into the cavern was slow. After twenty minutes of clambering down small cliffs and slipping between cracks in the wall, Elwood began to wonder if Marissa even knew the way back to the surface.

Every twist and turn of the cavern looked identical to him—a mess of orange rocks and jagged shadows flanked by walls of darkness ahead and behind. The rocky forma-tions clinging to the ceiling started to run together, each one looking more familiar than the last, and Elwood suddenly felt the weight of the earth above him pressing down. His chest felt tight.

Just as the words, "I think I could use some air," were bubbling up in his throat, the narrow passage of weeping walls began to widen. A few paces later, the three spelunkers found themselves at the entrance to a multi-chambered cavern. In the dim distance, Elwood could see the cave branch off into a dozen smaller cavities, all littered with speckled mushrooms that coated the damp floor like a bumpy carpet.

"Knew it," said Marissa.

Elwood actually felt relieved. If the guy was hunting mushrooms, this would've been the place to do it. That meant they were close, and *that* meant he was one step closer to being home, where he could enjoy a hot bath and a nice cup of tea.

The young archer held his torch a bit higher and tried to peer into the distant chambers. The flickering light barely put a dent in the darkness. Why would anyone come all this way for some fungus?

"Should we have a look around then?" He asked, taking a few steps deeper inside.

Marissa's hand shot up to meet his chest.

"Wait."

Her nose twitched with short, quick inhales.

"What is it?" Grizmo asked.

"I could be wrong," she started, scrunching her face, "But I think that's blood."

The elderly gnome scoffed and waved a dismissive hand toward her.

"Oh, please. Come now," he said, trotting forward. "You found the mushrooms; I'll give you that. But blood? Over all these spores? Iron deposits, most likely. Really, all that business with the troll last week must have you on edge. Hate Elwood and I missed that."

Marissa tried to interject, but Grizmo pushed past her.

"Let's think for a moment, shall we? If this place were dangerous, would the mushroom farmer keep coming back? No, of course he wouldn't. Now then, there's research to be done!"

Marissa's mouth flattened to a thin line. Elwood thought about backing her up, but once Grizmo's curiosity was piqued, there was little conversation to be had.

The balding gnome rifled through his pack and revealed—with as much pizazz as he could—an invention.

It was some kind of cap, which he happily strapped to his head. At its crest, a mechanical arm held an oversized magnifying glass, and he brought it down to rest a few inches from his face. He removed his glove, gave the cap a tap, and a bright blue light burst from the front of the glass. Grizmo then got down on all fours and peered at the blanket of mushrooms.

"Amazing," he sighed. "And to think, they flourish here without so much as a speck of sunlight. Fascinating, isn't it? Doesn't it make you wonder how they work?"

Marissa stalked off to the closest chamber and shined her torch inside it. Though Grizmo wasn't the least bit aware of it, Elwood could feel the tension brooding in the cave, and he did his best to smooth things over.

"I think that might just be you, big guy," he said with an awkward laugh. "Look, I know this is all very interesting, but don't you think we should—"

Elwood's voice caught in his throat. Wriggling its way along the damp stone behind Grizmo was a crusty, undulating tentacle. It reared back like a snake ready to strike.

"Griz—!"

The tentacle whipped forward, wrapping itself around the gnome's neck. With a single, sickening crunch, it yanked Grizmo's body into the darkness. His lantern and cap came loose in the assault, shattering against the cavern floor.

Marissa screamed and sprinted past Elwood into the shadows. With her blade drawn, she thrust her torch into the darkness around her.

"Grizmo? Grizmo! Say something!"

Blood rushed into Elwood's ears. The thump of his heartbeat nearly drowned out the elf's screams. He jammed his hand into his quiver and fumbled with it. With a clatter, the arrows spilled out onto the cavern floor, and he fell to his knees, scrambling to grab one. Elwood looked up in stunned horror, desperate to seat the arrow on the bowstring, but his trembling hands made it impossible.

From the darkness, a second tentacle lashed out, wrapped around Marissa's waist, and effortlessly plucked her into another dark chamber. Her torch spun in midair for a beat, then rattled to the floor. The flame winked out.

Elwood shot to his feet as a wet silence filled the cavern. At that exact moment, alone and shaking in the dark, he might have thought about running, about sprinting from the cavern and never looking back, but the idea wouldn't come to the front of his mind. That space was occupied by three thoughts that repeated endlessly.

He was wrong.

This *was* an adventure, after all.

And it was *definitely* not worth ten silver pieces.

INTO THE MOONMIRE

D eep inside the swamp, four lanterns floated like will-o'-wisps in the darkness. The deep orange flicker pressed against the night, penetrating the tree line and surrounding the four travelers in a glowing rib cage of swollen trunks and crooked limbs. With every step, the slurping and slapping of boots against muck grew louder, and the putrid, sulfurous stench of the bog wormed its way deeper into their nostrils.

From her position in the center of the pack, Lavender drew her cloak tight around her shoulders. Each huff of exertion carried with it a thick cloud of fog, and she watched as the steam danced into the air like a specter, haunting them from overhead before retreating into the shadows. She'd heard stories of the Moonmire, and thus far, it was living up to its reputation.

There was a shift then, slight and silent—the vaguest change in the wind. Lavender could feel it, clinging like static to the back of her neck, begging the hairs there to stand on end. She slowed her pace and sank ankle-deep into the reeking mud, peering into the blackness beyond the lantern light. The pale trees rose around her like fractured finger bones threatening to tighten their grip.

She knew this feeling. The weight in the air. The heat at her back and the chill that followed after.

They were being watched.

"Alright then, little one?" A voice called out, warm and dry as sawdust.

At the front of the pack, Barnabus turned to peer over his shoulder toward the little halfling scanning the darkness. In the shade of his wide-brimmed hat, and behind a long, bristly beard the color of pipe smoke, a gentle smile reached the wrinkles around his eyes.

"Something isn't right," Lavender said. "I had a strange feeling."

She turned to her left, peering at a spot where the light's edge seemed to collide with a solid wall of shadow. It was only for a blink, but she was certain of it. There was a glimmer—the kind that might appear as distant lantern light flashed against a set of black, glassy eyes. Something was there, and whatever she saw—saw her, too.

The others came to a squishy stop, signaling their growing impatience with heavy sighs. Barnabus ignored them and planted his knobby oaken staff into the grime. In the lanterns' glow, his layered robes shimmered like rubies.

"Perhaps we've been traveling too long, hm?" He asked. "A short rest might help ease your mind. I'm certain we could all use a quick sit down by a fire."

He rubbed his palms together, breathed a few puffs of warm air into them, then batted the fog away with a wizened hand.

"Not an option," Alberic said.

The armor-clad half-orc spoke with the tone of a captain, deep and commanding. He shifted his weight to one side and rested his hand over the pommel of a thick-bladed sword.

"There's no time. If we push on now, we can reach Evergate by mid-morning."

"He's right," Quinn said, her voice as rich and smooth as fine velvet and equally out of place in the mire. "I'd rather not stay here any longer than required."

"All the same," Barnabus said, "A few moments rest might do us some—"

"Quiet!" Lavender whisper-shouted. The little ranger had already nocked an arrow. "Listen."

Alberic heaved his sword from its sheath and rotated into a position between the halfling and the wizard, who had plucked his staff from the grime and was gripping it tightly with both hands. Quinn darted forward to join them, slipping two daggers from her hips and turning a long, elven ear toward the darkness.

"I hear nothing," she murmured.

"Exactly. The bugs? The birds? They've gone quiet. We're not alone," Lavender said.

Back to back, the four stood there, motionless, tight as a tendon ready to snap. They studied the trees in the silence, trying desperately to make out a shape, to tune into a sound —*something*. Not even the wind whispered in response. The static at the back of Lavender's neck now burned like lightning, sending waves of tremors down her legs.

The Moonmire was tightening its grip. The light felt dim and useless, and their quickened breaths summoned a cloud of apparitions that loomed overhead like guests at a wake.

A minute passed. Then another.

Alberic was the first to relax his shoulders.

"Maybe you were right, Barnabus. Perhaps we could use a rest," he said, letting out an embarrassed half-laugh. "I think this swamp has us all on—"

A violent rush of muck erupted from the nearby trees, dousing the party in a thick layer of putrid, brackish swamp water. Three of the lanterns went out in an instant, and the fourth flickered and hissed viciously, clinging to life. Quinn fumbled with it, and the water inside splashed against the glass.

"No, no, no, no!"

Then, the flame hissed for the last time, and a heavy, silent darkness swallowed them whole.

Lavender stared wide-eyed into the nothingness, an arrow drawn to her cheek. Her pupils danced around the void, slowly expanding, revealing one detail at a time.

The first was the shape of her hand, dripping with grime and white-knuckled around the grip of her short bow. The second was the shimmer of her arrowhead in the moonlight, which trembled and rattled in place.

Then, as the deep darkness gave way to layers of gray, she saw it. There, bathed in shadows within a mangled heap of downed trees and prickly thorns, was a face.

Two perfectly round eyes stared back at her, cold as glass and black as coal. They were surrounded by a halo of tightly packed white feathers, like those of a barn owl, but the visage was as wide as a man's torso. But it wasn't the face itself that made the halfling's heart claw its way up through her throat to choke the breath from her.

"Is that... a bird?" Barnabus asked. He squinted and leaned toward it.

He couldn't see it—couldn't make out the shape in the darkness. Lavender wanted to scream—to warn them— but only a weak clicking sound came out.

Beyond the expressionless face in the brush, the rest of the creature's monstrous form towered over the brambles. Beneath its feathered head and neck stood a human-like torso, furless and gaunt, heaving slightly with careful, silent breaths. A set of ram's horns coiled out from its head like a twisted crown, and a pair of tattered, leathery wings sat perched in the dark, perfectly placed within the shadows, ready to propel it skyward.

Lavender's nose caught a whiff of something on the wind—a stench that crept its way deep into the back of her throat and dwarfed the reek of the bog. Something foul and rotten and snake-like. She pried her eyes from the creature ahead.

Two more sets of eyes. These were smaller and lower to the ground. Their wings were pinned back and tight against their withered forms, but their blackened claws were dug deep into the trees, ready to hurl themselves headlong toward the soaking party. All they needed was a moment.

Alberic waved his sword overhead, slicing the moonlight and shouting, "Hey! Get out of here! Go!"

Lavender turned in horror, but her voice remained locked in her throat. The knight pounded his armored chest and made himself as big as he could. He hollered into the dark, taking two big steps forward. And then, the screeching started.

THE HOLE

The Whisperwood is a shadowy place, a sprawling mess of tangled branches and twisted trunks where the light must squeeze its way toward the forest floor like water through tightly bound fingers. Here, the near-still wind sings in an ancient tongue, foreboding hymns that hang stagnant in the air and fall harmless on ears that have forgotten how to listen.

It is a place of life, as all forests are known to be, but one wrapped in layers of decay and neglect. Mushrooms carpet the darkest regions, spewing choking spores that reek of mildew and wet burlap, and the fauna here have grown skittish with time, having heard the warnings on the wind, whose language they still yet speak.

The creatures of the wood move without sound, patiently stalking the brush with razor claws and wide-set eyes accustomed to the persistent gloom. Birds do not sing here. The crickets dare not chirp.

It is a pervasive quiet that haunts the Whisperwood, where twig snaps and falling nuts scream like thunderclaps in the stillness. Rivers and streams run thick with moss and poison snakes, and the fruit trees bear misshapen things with blackened peels and bitter flesh.

It is a spellbinding place and terrible all the same, entirely uninhabited by man or elf, who have long known the dangers that lie within. Only the Whisper Gnomes reside within the woods' crooked halls and endless dim. They have forgotten much of the world beyond—the brightness of a noonday sun, the sound of laughing bellies, the cool touch of heavy rain. Their skin and locks have grayed with time, and their eyes have changed, now icy and colorless things that see much and express little.

The Whisper Gnomes are reclusive creatures, fiercely protective of their dwellings but not often likely to extend their reach beyond the gnarled doors of their woodland keeps. They are regarded as myth more often than not, and few travelers have had the luck (or lack thereof) to catch glimpses of them in the shade. Those that claim as much are routinely hushed or brushed aside as fibbers and exaggerators.

In truth, it had been nearly ten years since the last sighting of a Whisper Gnome. That is, until one day when Jimothy Toeshine III marched into the wood.

Jimothy was rather quiet for a halfling, sullen even, at least according to those who knew him best, which is to say one or two folks. He spoke little and shared the thoughts hidden behind his pale eyes even less. His perceived shyness, while not necessarily conducive to hospitality or companionship, did offer its own set of advantages, though.

Perhaps most notably, what his days lacked in conversation, they made up for in productivity. It is amazing how much one can accomplish when unburdened by the small talk of everyday people. It can be assumed that this diligence was how Jimothy became the youngest Button Knight in his Order's history, but it did little in the way of helping the halfling establish friendships, which, were you to ask and were he to answer, was fine by him.

Perhaps then it will come as no surprise that, on this day, the little knight found himself alone at the edge of the Whisperwood. His leather armor was polished to a near mirror-like finish, and his two short swords (which a human might mistake for simple kitchen knives) were razor sharp and affixed tightly to his belt. His bag was packed with provisions, his boots were laced symmetrically, and his mind was set on making his way through the tangled wild before him.

He had little time to spare, so he wasted none whatsoever. Without so much as a glance toward the safety of the village in the meadow behind him, Jimothy strode forward, crossed the threshold of the wood, and was plunged into twilight.

There are no simple paths through the Whisperwood. For three days and two nights, Jimothy navigated the tangled roots and winding paths of the forest. Dusk and dawn were hardly distinguishable in the ever-shade, and without so much as starlight to guide his route, the going was slow and noisy. Each step of his little feet echoed like shattered glass in an empty chapel.

After the second day, he referenced his map for the final time, stuffing it deep within his pack and cursing whichever cartographer alleged its accuracy. He should have known better. No one had ever explored the Whisper-wood in its entirety, much less made a record of the ever-changing paths and streams that writhed their way through the underbrush.

He climbed over hills and crawled under briars, choked his way through odiferous mushroom patches, and forded fast-moving rapids. When the sun rose on the third day (or at least by the time it finally made its presence known, which was likely late into morning), Jimothy knew beyond all reasonable doubt that he was totally and helplessly lost. So far as the halfling could tell, he could've been walking in one winding circle. Each mangled tree trunk looked more familiar than the last, and no matter which way he spun, the sun seemed to glow like a dull blanket over the whole canopy, not one spot any brighter than another.

He had few options now. Returning to the village was impossible, or at least no more possible than finding his way to the other side of the forest. He could try climbing to the top of the canopy, but the skeletal limbs of the surrounding trees did not seem so strong, even for a climber of his little weight.

If he were to try it, he'd need to remove his armor first, and that wasn't an option. He'd felt the heat of predators' eyes on his back since he first entered the forest, and though they'd yet to reveal themselves, he would do nothing to expose himself any more than a being of his stature already was.

He chose instead to press on a bit further, but as one familiar sight gave way to another, Jimothy grew weary. He had slept little over the last three days, and the panic in his heart pulled the fatigue over his shoulders like a warm, heavy quilt.

Up ahead, bathed in a rare spotlight of pure sun, was a cradle of roots at the base of an ancient maple. The blackened leaves there seemed to call to him, inviting him in for a short nap. Just for a moment.

He offered no resistance. As he nestled into the roots and foliage, a soft breeze caressed his face, and before long, his eyelids fell heavy against his cheeks. Then, all was dark in the Whisperwood.

The sharp snap of a single twig erupted in Jimothy's ear— a snare drum in a narrow cave. Jolted awake, the halfling shot up, but as his neck pressed into something sharp, he froze. The twilight had deepened to a fiery orange at the approach of dusk, and in the burning dim, the halfling found that he was surrounded on all sides by creatures not much bigger than himself.

They were gnomes, or similar enough, each with charcoal armor and capes the color of day-old snow. Many were armed with twisting, vine-like bows, and three dozen arrows were drawn and aimed at his cradle beneath the tree.

Two of the creatures, which Jimothy could only assume were the fabled folk of the Whisperwood, stepped aside, allowing an older man to step forward. This gnome wore more elegant armor, and his short beard came into a perfect point beneath his chin. His hair was the color of quartz, and it laid flat against his head without a single strand out of place. In his hands was a maple twig, snapped in two at its exact center.

The old man said nothing. He simply peered down his hooked nose at the halfling, analyzing the little knight's every feature with cold, frosted eyes.

After some time, he looked to a gnome standing above Jimothy's right shoulder—the one with an arrow trained on his ear—then gave a single, curt nod. The next moment, something rough and thick was pulled down hard over the halfling's head. Ungentle hands yanked him from the forest floor, and he was off. But to where, he didn't know.

Discerning time from inside a potato sack is no simple task, but the halfling did his best. For days, Jimothy was led deeper into the woods. His hot breath grew sticky inside the bag, clinging to his cheeks and filling his nose with an awful odor. Sometimes he would be forced, wordlessly, to sit on the lumpy ground to rest. Other times he would be spun around over and again, first clockwise, then counter, until his head swam and his knees grew weak. He assumed this was to prevent him from knowing the path, which seemed altogether silly for an already hopelessly lost captive with a sack over his head.

Each day, after many hours of clumsy marching, he would be pushed over entirely, as if being told to sleep. Minutes later, the soft rumble of snoring would grow from the several dozen mouths around him, and Jimothy would slowly drift off to join them.

He thought, more than once and especially just before

dreaming, about slipping from his restraints and fleeing. But to where? His weapons and pack were taken, his belly was all but empty, and he had absolutely no idea where he was (not that he had before, mind you).

He grew more restless and more exhausted with each labored step. Every now and then, the gnomes lifted the bag above his lips and offered him a sip of water from a canteen or a bite of something dry and dusty. It did little to fight off the hunger, but he found himself with just enough energy to keep his little legs moving. During these moments of rest, the silence grew deafening, a blaring alarm in the stillness.

Not once during the many days together did the gnomes utter a single word. It was a silent march, apart from the muffled crunching of leaves beneath the halfling's feet and the sound of the bag scratching against his ears. Shortly after the journey began, Jimothy had worked up the courage to question his captors.

"Where are you taking me?"

There was a moment of stillness as the gnomes seemed to halt. Then, in a flurry of movement, a dozen blunt objects sank into his torso, smashing into his stomach and across his back, again and again. Jimothy fell to the forest floor, gasping and rigid. He didn't try to speak again after that.

On what he guessed to be the sixth night in the Whisperwood, Jimothy was not given the luxury of sleep. Around the time he expected to be forced to the ground to rest, the company picked up its pace. Several times, Jimothy was hoisted aloft and carried over what felt like difficult terrain, only to be tossed back to the ground and shoved forward once again.

Hours later, a slight glow appeared within the bag. It must've been morning. A rough hand clamped down upon his shoulder, commanding him to stop. Then, he heard new sounds.

Papers shuffling. Canvas tarps being lifted and set aside. Wet boots against carpet. A palm pressed against his back and pushed him forward, where he stumbled onto something soft. Then, in a flash, the sack was ripped from his head.

The twilight was blinding after so many days in the bag, and he blinked hard until the blurry world grew clear. He was in a tent. Not a simple camping tent, but rather like a war tent with high ceilings and canvas walls upon which maps and decorative curtains were hung. In the center of the room was a wide wooden table littered with books and papers and candles and drawings. There were chairs, weapon racks, and all manner of other furnishings spread about the place, as well as a sheet-covered object with a round upper edge.

Behind the central table, an aging gnome with ashy skin and ivory hair sat in a plush and colorless armchair. His pale lips were wrapped tightly around the bit of an ebony pipe, and a pair of half-moon reading glasses sat at the very tip of his nose.

He eyed Jimothy with a sharp, indignant gaze that seemed to pierce through the halfling's armor to peer at his naked soul. The elder gnome took exactly two puffs from his pipe and let out a silent smoke ring that rolled through the tent air before colliding against the roof. He then exchanged a long, wordless look with a nearby soldier. The subject of his attention, a young lady in silvery armor, seemed to receive the message. She gave a single nod in response before striding toward Jimothy, who was forced to his knees before the elder's table.

The lady gnome carried an intricately carved bowl in her hands, and though Jimothy couldn't see what it contained, the smell of sour herbs and oils filled his nose. She jammed two fingers into something wet inside, then reached out and, with a not-so-gentle touch, painted something along his forehead. With a final dot between his eyes, the tent came alive with sound.

Voices. Laughter. Conversations. Dozens of them, thin as smoke and distant as the moon. Jimothy looked about the place, but not a single gnome's lips were moving. They stood still and silent, yet their voices echoed inside his skull.

The elder leaned over the table's edge and tamped his pipe.

"You can hear me, yes?"

His mouth remained closed, but his voice pressed like ice into Jimothy's brain. It was cold and clear, trailing into his thoughts like a glacier.

"I can," the stunned halfling spoke aloud.

At this, each of the creatures in the tent winced in unison, and for a brief moment, the wispy conversation stopped altogether. Even the presumed leader's eye twitched at the sound.

"Ah, ah," the gnome spoke again within Jimothy's mind. "Inside voices. *Inside* voices."

He gently tapped the side of his head.

Jimothy focused on the leader and repeated himself.

"I can," he thought.

The symbol upon Jimothy's forehead grew warm as the words left his mind.

"Splendid."

A thin smile tugged at the edges of the gnome's lips as he sat back and drew from the pipe once again.

"Who are you?"

"I could ask you the same," Jimothy thought.

The gnome exhaled through his nostrils, and a cloud of pungent tobacco smoke surrounded his face. His crystal eyes still pierced into Jimothy's.

"I will not ask again," he said.

"Jimothy Toeshine III. Junior Button Knight."

"And why have you come here?"

"*You* brought me here," the halfling thought. He did little to disguise his tone.

The gnome took a steady breath.

"To the *Whisperwood*."

"I was passing through. Nothing more. On the third day, I realized I was lost. Not long after, your people ambushed me, and now we're here. That's the entire story."

"Not many are foolish enough to wander here, let alone by themselves. You are either incredibly brave or incredibly stupid."

The gnome's voice gripped Jimothy's mind like a frozen claw.

"Certainly one of the two. Though, by the look of things, I'm beginning to believe it's the latter," Jimothy thought.

"I hope, for your sake, it is the former."

At this, the gnome rose from his chair, circled the table, and dispensed several silent orders. The next moment, Jimothy's bindings were cut, his swords were returned, and he was brought to his feet.

"You have given me your name, so I shall give you mine in return. Hask. Commander Hask. You, Jimothy Toeshine III, have committed a crime. You are a trespasser."

The halfling hung on the gnome's every word within his mind. He'd been returned his belongings, and freedom felt but a sentence away. Why, then, was this commander laying out his crimes? Hask's words flowed into Jimothy's thoughts like chilled molasses, and he wished more than anything that the gnome would deliver them more swiftly.

"There are punishments for crimes such as yours," the commander continued. "It is within our right to imprison you in the Murmuring Keep, and it is within our power to leave your lifeless husk to the creatures of the wood. We could strip you of your garb and send you headlong into the wilds or remove your tongue from your mouth, reminding you daily of the silence of the lands you dared to enter uninvited."

So far, none of the options were what Jimothy would consider ideal.

"Then again, there is another option," said Hask.

"I do hope this one involves keeping my life," Jimothy thought.

"That I cannot say," Hask replied. "Not for certain. You are strong to come here. Stronger still to survive the march to this place. Perhaps that strength will serve you well."

Commander Hask circled behind the wooden table, relit his pipe, and studied the collection of parchment splayed out before him. Jimothy approached but found the letters and maps scribed in a language he didn't recognize.

"There are strange happenings in the Whisperwood, Jimothy." Hask's voice was no longer so sharp, and it trickled into Jimothy's mind like snow beneath a new spring sun. "We would like you to investigate. Should you survive, you may take your leave—your crimes forgiven, and your face now welcome within our halls."

Jimothy thought for a long time. He could feel the commander's impatient, frosty gaze upon him, but the halfling was not so quick to cut deals with those he did not yet fully trust.

"What kind of strange happenings?" He thought.

"I will show you."

Commander Hask strode to the right side of the tent and approached the large oval-shaped and sheet-covered object. In one swift motion, he plucked the fabric free and let it fall to the carpet below. It was a mirror, or rather, it had been at one time. The reflective surface in its center was missing, and hovering there, in the empty space within the golden frame, was something Jimothy didn't quite understand.

It was a portal—a hole in space that swirled and shimmered like liquid emerald. The oblong rift was not much bigger than a Whisper Gnome, and it released a low hum as it undulated there in the mirror frame. The little knight stared into its depths, lost in the pattern.

"I would very much like to help you," Jimothy thought, "But I'm afraid I know little of the arcane. I doubt I would be of much use with something like this. Now, if it were a creature you needed slaying or—"

The commander's voice shot into his mind like frozen shears, snipping his train of thought in two.

"You misunderstand, boy."

Jimothy peeled his gaze away from the vortex. Commander Hask stood tall, still as a statue, delivering an icy glare in his direction that shot deep into the halfling's core. His soul once again felt violated, and he became suddenly aware that the other soldiers had formed a tight circle at his back.

"This is not a request, Jimothy Toeshine III. This is a punishment, remember? Now..." Commander Hask took an authoritative step forward.

A light breeze brushed against the beads of sweat collecting atop Jimothy's brow, and a chill found its way to his knees, which shook beneath his armor. As slow as snowfall, Hask extended a pale finger toward the thrumming portal.

"Get in the hole."

THE ALL-CLERIC

It was a quiet evening in the Two-Tusk Inn and a good one at that. Beneath the light of a wrought iron chandelier, a dwarven bard sat in a deep violet doublet, lightly plucking away at a lute, rocking in time with the cheerful notes. The sound swept through the hall, washing over the shiplap walls and dancing across the timeworn tabletops.

When the melodies faded between songs, a murmuring could be heard from the little pockets of well-traveled guests. They were all hunched up around tables, sipping steaming drinks and gazing at the fire crackling in the hearth. There was the occasional toast—a giggle here, a sneeze there—but all in all, it was rather peaceful, just the way Barry the barkeep liked it.

The balding half-orc behind the counter was more than happy to make himself seem busy. He lazily wiped down a glass and hummed an off-key tune that hardly matched the one coming from the little stage at the back. Every once in a while, he'd stop to take a gander around the room, refill a patron's glass, or brush a few errant crumbs from the apron that clung to his round belly. Soon after, he'd pick up the same glass and keep polishing away. It didn't matter that it had been clean for the last half hour.

A little brass bell chimed above the entrance to the inn, followed by the low howl of frigid wind. Barry peeked around one of the many wooden posts that rose toward the ceiling, expecting to see one of his regulars, ready to deliver the same warm welcome he'd already given so many times that night. This time, however, it was a stranger that shuffled in from the blustery snow, and Barry found himself more than a little puzzled at the sight.

A short, stocky man in a plain brown coat waddled into the inn, ushered inside by a thick flurry of white powder. He shut the door behind him, removed his hood, shook his shoulders free of the snowflakes, and shivered once from top to bottom. The top of the stranger's head was shiny bald, but the outside was packed with thick white curls, like a sheep that was several seasons overdue for a good sheering.

It wasn't the man's features or clothes that left Barry silent, though. It was the jewelry. His neck was wreathed in layers of pendants, chains, and pearls. Large baubles and trinkets hung above his round belly, and each of his fingers was packed with rings. His wrists shook with a dozen bracelets each, and his ankles were piled high with gold and silver hoops in much the same way. He even wore two bandoliers across his chest, each adorned with little wooden statues and other knickknacks.

The stranger wobbled and jangled his way to the bar (which he disappeared beneath for a moment), tossed down his satchel, and wiggled his way on top of the stool. After shuffling his bottom into a comfy spot and waiting for the jewelry to cease its clanging, he looked up to Barry with a tired smile.

"Good evening then," he said in a sleepy voice. "Something warm or strong, if you please. Both, if you have it."

Barry crossed his arms and raised an eyebrow. "A good evening it is, stranger. Welcome to the Two-Tusk Inn. The name's Barry."

"A pleasure," the man said.

Barry looked the stranger up and down, studying the baubles. They weren't simple trinkets or jewelry after all. They were holy symbols. Dozens of them.

All of them.

Each piece that laid against the man's snow-crusted coat was adorned with a symbol—skulls and swords, hammers and eyes, stars and leaves. There were crosses and horns on many of his rings, while wings and flames were etched into the bangles. Little statues peeped from the pockets of his bandoliers, all tiny caricatures of deities and demigods. Some were well-known, and others Barry didn't recognize at all.

The barkeep cleared his throat. "You know I have to ask, right?"

"I suspected as much." The man swallowed and wet his lips. He was still smiling, but it no longer reached his eyes.

"Tell you what," said Barry, resting an elbow on the bar. "You tell me about," he vaguely motioned at the man's torso, "all *that*, and the first round's on me. We have us a deal?"

The stranger looked away and nodded, resting his gaze on the snowfall beyond the window. With each flurry that brushed against the frosted glass, his smile crept closer to a thin, flat line. After a minute, Barry thought he might've reconsidered the offer, but just like that, the man started to speak.

"The world out there, Barry—beyond that glass..." He trailed off. "It's dangerous. Far more so than you might think, and I've seen my fair share of it. Word is, I've earned a bit of a reputation for," he mirrored the vague gesture toward his body, "All this."

"My name is Aldwyn Finch. Or it was, at some point or another. Nowadays, most folks just call me the All-Cleric." He glanced up then, giving a shallow shrug. The charms and chains jingled with the motion. "Well, if the robes fit, eh?"

Aldwyn shot a finger toward a pot of steaming mulled wine behind the counter, and Barry obliged, wordlessly filling a tankard as the cleric continued.

"There are so many wonderful things to see out there," he said, tossing a knobby thumb toward the wall of windows. "But, there's also a great deal of unpleasantness to be found. Some might call it evil, but I believe that word gets thrown around too lightly. People use evil to make sense of misfortune. They point to evil to say, 'If this awful thing happened, it must've happened for a reason.' The fact of the matter is that most of life's unpleasantness doesn't need a reason. You can stumble into unpleasantness wherever you go. Just walk behind a well-fed horse for long enough."

"But *evil*? Evil doesn't happen by accident. Evil takes work. You need a daily itinerary if you want to be properly evil. That's why most things out there settle for being *bad* instead. Nevertheless, people often struggle to tell the difference between the two. In my experience, evil is rare. Bad is abundant."

"It hides in the shadows and creeps beneath the trees. Sometimes it waits in caverns or slithers along the sand. Bad things come in all shapes and sizes and flavors. Some want to stomp you or eat you, others want to trick you or chase you, and some don't seem to want at all. It's just in their nature, I suppose—to choke, and scratch, and bite, and smash. From my perspective, regardless of what things might want, it's all bad news for me, and I don't *want* much to do with any of it."

Aldwyn paused then, watching as the snow continued to collect in the corners of the windowsill like little mountains. Barry slid a steaming tankard toward him, and the cleric clasped it with both hands. Then he looked down and adjusted one of the many baubles along his chest.

"To tell you the truth, Barry, my journey thus far has been little else but claws, and teeth, and wings, and fire."

He stared into the half-orc's apron and nodded deeply. "A great deal of fire."

The barkeep leaned against the counter behind him and crossed his arms again, scrunching his face up.

"It sounds like you've had quite the adventure, my friend. But that doesn't really answer my question. Why all the—"

"Ah, yes," Aldwyn cut him off. "You wanted to know why I wear all this, didn't you? It's quite simple, really."

The All-Cleric raised his tankard of wine in a half-hearted toast and gave Barry a tired wink.

"Because I'll take all the help I can get."

The Cinder

Chamomile Tenpenny sat beneath a curtain of shimmering starlight. Nestled in the bend of a silvery sand dune, the little halfling stoked the crackling campfire at her feet and watched as the embers spiraled upward, dancing like a whirl of fireflies to join the millions of glittering pinpricks overhead. It was as if the whole universe were spread out before her.

The sky here had given up on its façade, choosing now to reveal its true self to Chamomile for the first time. It was not so empty and dark at all, she thought. In fact, there were a great many colors to be found up above: Layers of twisting violet and deep blues, splashes of scarlet and swirls of turquoise. Each hue rolled into the next, all gleaming and spotless, as if the Lightmaker herself had dusted the scene with glitter.

A stiff breeze rolled across the sand and found its way into Chamomile's nook. She trembled, breathed a puff of humid air into her palms, and held them out toward the flames. The books had warned her about the heat—this particular stretch of nothingness was called The Cinder, after all—but they'd failed to mention the chill that sets in when the sun dips below the horizon. Now, she sat there shivering, alone, and utterly infested with sand.

But it wasn't all bad, of course. She had the sky above to gaze into, and the dusty dunes that stretched out before her were bathed in the brightest moonlight that any halfling from any time had ever seen, and that was nothing to complain about. It was quiet here, apart from the crackle of twigs and the brush of sand as it plumed from the dune tops. If it weren't for the trembling, she might even call it peaceful.

Chamomile was deep in thought, lost in a twirl of particularly dense starlight, when a nearby shriek split the stillness of the night. Like a jagged blade, the sound tore her from the sky, and she scrambled to her feet at once, pulling the tiny mace from her hip and holding it aloft.

Beyond the flickering campfire, two shapes appeared at the top of the dune. They tripped and tumbled over the edge, sliding down the steep slope in a sheet of glistening sand. Between the fire and the moonlight, Chamomile could just make out their forms.

They were small creatures, not much bigger than the halfling herself, covered in dull red scales from horned head to clawed toe. Each wore something akin to an old flour sack over their torsos, and the makeshift garments were cinched tight against their thin bellies with frayed ropes.

One of them spotted Chamomile, and their slitted, reptilian eyes went so wide it looked as if they might pop from their bony face. They scrambled towards her, clawing desperately at the sand, and stammering in a language that vaguely resembled the one Chamomile spoke.

"P-p-p-please… he-help…" Each sound flailed from their toothy mouth between sharp, labored gulps of air.

The halfling lowered her mace and took a quick step backward as the creature snatched at her robe.

"Slow down there," she said. "What's wrong? What happened?"

By now, the one lagging behind had caught up, and they both knelt before her, backs heaving and limbs trembling. The one speaking did not look up at her. Instead, they shut their eyes tight, gripping the sand with both hands until it crunched loudly between their claws.

"We... dig... sand..." They tried to explain.

"You were digging somewhere?" Chamomile asked.

The creature nodded furiously. "We... find... a... thing..."

The halfling cocked her head to one side. "What did you—"

"Bad," they cut her off. "Some... bad."

"Run," the other added.

"We... run," the first continued. "Three... days... no... water..."

"You've been running for three days? Out here?"

She noticed then, for the first time, how tightly their skin clung to their bones, the chapped flesh around their eyes and nostrils. She looked away, choosing instead to scan the edges of the dune for movement.

"What exactly did you find?"

There was no response. After a moment, Chamomile looked down to find one of the creatures burying their snout into the sand. Their hands were crossed behind their head, and their tail was stuck straight into the air. The other was flat on their rump, stiff as a board, with one clawed finger extended toward something behind her.

Their lower jaw was flapping, but not even a trace of a whisper escaped.

Chamomile gripped her mace a little tighter. The fright of their shrieking arrival had only just subsided, but now her heart was beating against her breastbone again, a loose crate in the back of a speeding wagon. With the sound thumping in her ears, she turned—slowly—and peered into the darkness.

The fire was stretching her shadow into a long, gangly form that traveled along the sand and disappeared over the edge of the dune. There, right where it met the sky, was the silhouette of a gaunt, malformed figure. Its limbs were loosely wrapped in ancient, filthy linens that dangled from its skeletal frame like entrails. What little moonlit flesh could be seen was dried and blackened, and its slack jaw hung low—too low—against its chest. There was no tongue inside it. Nothing but a leathery maw of bleach-white teeth with a dark hole at the back.

Chamomile hardly noticed these details, though. She was much too busy staring into the set of glowing, putrid-green eyes gleaming back at her in the moonlight. The creature arched its back, took a lumbering step forward, and unleashed a dusty, hollow moan that seemed to collect in the back of Chamomile's skull like a sad memory.

As it shambled down the slope, the halfling's shoulders relaxed.

"Oh, thank the Lightmaker," she sighed. "That's not so bad."

She broke eye contact with the tatter-wrapped thing

across from her, knelt down by her worn leather pack, and started rummaging through pockets and opening pouches.

"Tell me I remembered to restock the holy water," she grumbled.

Just as she was elbow deep into the bag's main compartment, one of the scaly creatures beside her finally managed to cough out a single word.

"Run."

"Run?" She asked. "I thought you'd be tired of running by now. Here. Drink this."

She plucked a waterskin from the bag and held it out. They took it with a trembling claw, then whipped their head back toward the approaching figure.

"Don't worry about them," Chamomile said. "I'll take care of that. I just need to find—there we go."

She pulled a stained scroll out of her pack and began untying the red ribbon around its center.

"I was hoping to save this for something a bit bigger, but," she shrugged.

"It..." The scaly creature whined.

"I know. Getting a bit close, isn't it?"

And it was. The shambling figure was now halfway to them. Its arms were coiled up against its chest, and its torso writhed in sharp, unnatural jerks. The moaning grew louder, and its exposed teeth snapped together with a *clack, clack, clack*.

"Just look at me and drink your water," Chamomile said.

"But—"

"No buts, my friend." She shook her head. "Oh, I never caught your name. Actually, hold that thought."

She unrolled the scroll and held it vertically in front of her. The figure was almost upon them, eyes burning and teeth gnashing. Chamomile glanced over her shoulder at the two creatures behind her—the ones trembling violently in the sand.

"Don't be scared," she said. "But you might want to close your eyes for this next part."

They did so. Just as the horror came within striking distance of Chamomile, just as the musty stench of its ancient wraps filled her nose, just as it reared back to rake its withered claws down upon her, the little cleric took a single step forward and read the scroll.

If there had been a caravan in the desert that night, and if they had been many miles away and looking to the horizon, they would have witnessed something truly spectacular: A column of radiant light that glistened like millions of diamonds suspended in liquid pearl. The pillar burst from the Cinder floor and rose into the stars overhead, as if it were meant to hold up the very night sky itself.

Even with her eyelids shut, Chamomile's vision went white as she stood bathed in a pillar of radiance as warm as the summer sun and as gentle as snowfall. There was a slight sizzling sound, followed by the gasps of the little creatures behind her. Chamomile felt the scroll in her hands disintegrate, and a moment later, the light slowly faded from the desert.

When she opened her eyes again, the tattered horror was nowhere to be found. Only a small plume of glowing embers remained, and the desert wind gently lifted them into the sky like the sparks of a little campfire. Before long, the cinders disappeared altogether—nothing more than stardust.

Chamomile stood quietly once again, lost in the view, feeling warm for the first time all night. The two creatures behind her slowly approached, passing the waterskin back and forth and taking big gulps of air between their turns to drink.

The one who had done most of the talking took a spot beside Chamomile and joined her in looking up at the stars.

"My name... is Zara," they said.

Chamomile smiled. "That's pretty."

It was then that the little creature found the same swirling patch of starlight that Chamomile had been so fond of all night. They smiled, too.

"Pretty."

THE BRUSH PILE

"Curse that Johnald Greenhill! That no good, furry-footed, half-drunk, no-tooth-havin' son of a hag!"

The Gilded Gopher was, by all accounts, a typically tranquil, happy-go-lucky sort of tavern in a not-so-famous village somewhere between no place special and the middle of nowhere. On any given day, patrons would wander in here and there, have a sit down by the hearth, and enjoy a pint or three. It was a happy place, arguably the perfect place to wind down at the end of a busy day, sing a few songs, and forget one's worries. Today, however, was the exception to that rule.

Poplin Tinkertot was on another level. Now several ales into his furious monologue, the tawny wrinkles around the old gnome's features had twisted and contorted into something like a fingerprint. It hardly resembled a face at all. With every barb and swear, his skin grew redder until his whole head looked like the eye of an angry volcano threatening to spew hellfire and hot ash onto anyone within shouting distance.

His fury was the kind for which there is no remedy apart from getting it all out, so the other patrons waited silently and stared at the ripples in their mugs. With gusto, Poplin repeatedly stamped his little foot into the floorboards, unleashing a seemingly never-ending flurry of colorful curses and profanity at Johnald's expense.

"Two weeks, I asked him! For *two weeks*, I've been beggin' that low down, prune-faced, sorry spawn of a harpy to help me cut back the brush on my property line—and what happens?!"

The bartender, who was dutifully counting a collection of spoons in a poor attempt to seem busy, could have sworn she saw steam trickling from the gnome's ears. Poplin pounded down whatever was left in his glass and sent it flying clear across the room, where it shattered against the wall. Compared to the shouting just before, it was a quiet, muffled sort of sound.

"We're there all of ten minutes. *Ten minutes!* I go off to grab another hoe, and the next thing I know, poof! He's up and left. Gone! Skedaddled! Vanished! Not a trace to be found. And if I didn't know any better, I'd swear that brush pile was bigger than it was to begin with!"

But there *was* a trace to be found.

At the edge of town, just beyond the border of The Grainfields, there stood a little rock wall against the tree line. The stones had been brushed smooth with time, and little patches of moss had found cozy homes there within its cracks. Where this wall ended, a fence began, and little posts of weathered hardwood ran in semi-regular intervals all the way up to Poplin's house at the top of the hill. The barbed wire strung between the posts sagged in places and rusted in others, but it did the job well enough.

Just beyond the fence, the forest leaned up against the pasture, and great big limbs stretched out overtop the grass as if waking from a long summer nap. Here, at the edge of the wood, the little shrubs and vines of the forest floor had grown up into a lumbering, mangled heap. There were sticks and mushrooms and leaves and thorns, all twisted together in what some might mistake for a burn pile.

Only a few feet away were Poplin's tools: A shovel and a rake, a lantern and a rusty set of sheers, two hoes, and a red wheelbarrow with a half-flat tire. In his wrath, the old gnome hadn't bothered to wheel them all back up to his garden shed. Instead, he marched straight to The Gilded Gopher, where at this precise moment he was letting all the other guests know exactly what he thought of Johnald's mother.

But there was something else there. Something that Poplin overlooked.

It was a set of small footprints. They were pressed into the soft dirt there, just beside an upright shovel that stuck out of the ground. The tracks did not lead deeper into the woods, nor did they head back to town, or anywhere else for that matter. It was only the one pair, the kind that might appear if an old halfling stood in one place for too long, waiting patiently for his neighbor to return.

Beyond the fence line, there was a rustling. The brush pile shifted, so slightly that a nearby robin didn't bother to stop preening itself to have a look. All was still for a moment and quiet except for the grumbling buzz of bumblebees and the occasional verse from a nearby songbird. The heap shifted again, this time with a jerk.

Then it belched, and a multi-colored handkerchief shot from the pile and lazily floated to the ground by the shovel.

The Moonmire air hummed with the drone of a cricket choir and the sharp buzz of too many mosquitoes. A golden sunset poured in through the limbs overhead, painting the muddy waters in layers of burnt orange and ocher. There, a few ripples rolled and stretched along the surface as a creaking, swollen raft carrying five passengers crept its way toward a rare patch of somewhat-dry land.

The party's guide was named Gonga. He stood tall like a man, but his head was like that of a crocodile. Leathery scales covered his body from snout to webbed toes, and a thick tail trailed in the water behind him. With a clawed hand, Gonga steered the raft toward the muddy mound, where it sank into the sludge with a thick slurping sound. He hoisted a canvas satchel over his back and turned with a cold, reptilian expression toward the left side of the raft, where a young druidess sat whispering to a small chipmunk peeking out from her breast pocket.

"It is not very dry," Gonga said in his croaky, monotonous tone.

Aria looked up and gave a shrug. The chipmunk ducked out of sight.

"I'm sure it will be fine. Thank you, Gonga," Aria said.

The lizard stared blankly. "A fire will keep the biting things away."

Without blinking, he then plodded his way toward the center of the muddy island.

With Gonga's eyes no longer on her, Aria shivered.

"It's the voice," Adelphi said in a hushed tone. The sorceress shuffled toward Aria and took a seat beside her. She shot a wary glance toward their guide. "Still gives me the creeps."

"You get used to it," another flat voice said.

This one came from Tumbo, the red-scaled lizard merchant that accompanied them. He stared at the two of them with glassy, unfeeling eyes. Aria and Adelphi's faces flushed, and they shot up from their bench to gather their things. They quickly tied their robes up around their knees in fat knots and did their best to stretch over the muddiest parts of the island's edge. Tumbo blinked sideways.

"Why did their skin change color?" He asked the beard-less dwarf at the front of the boat.

"Couldn't tell ya," Umrick said, busily packing arrows into his quiver. "You should go ask them."

Tumbo, who thought nothing of the muck and could not comprehend sarcasm, plodded after the girls, droning, "Why did your skin change color?"

The dwarf grinned and flung his bow over his shoulder. The oozing mud stared back at him, and his grin quickly turned to a scowl. His stocky legs were too short to lunge over the foulest bits, so he didn't bother trying. By the time he reached the others, his armor was thickly crusted with sour-smelling mud from the knees down, and it squished inside his boots with each step.

Making camp was messy business. By the end of it, the

tents were smattered with sludge and the party was reasonably filthy. But there was a nice fire now and far fewer mosquitoes, and that was something. When the sun finally dipped behind the tree line, the Moonmire was swallowed by a damp, deep darkness. A second chorus began, this one comprised of frogs and birds and other less knowable things.

While Adelphi kept herself busy attending to a pot of bubbling stew, the others found what little comfort they could in a moment's rest. They reclined on long log benches and smoked their boots over the flames, occasionally swatting at the grape-sized flies that buzzed about.

With the steady hands of a jeweler, Umrick sat picking clods of mud from every ring of his chainmail. Every now and again, he'd lift his head and cut his eyes toward the darkness beyond the island. The trees groaned and swayed in the summer breeze, dancing like crooked teeth against an inky curtain of black.

Dotted here and there in the shadows were clusters of watchful eyes, little red and yellow orbs that glimmered in the firelight. One set would silently blink away, only for another to appear someplace else. Umrick shifted a little more with each new pair.

He picked a gnarly clump of clay from his armor and tossed it to the swamp floor. "What do you think's out there?"

"All sorts of things," said Aria, tossing a palmful of berries into her mouth. "Snakes. Spiders. Big cats. The usual things you might expect. Alligators."

Tumbo and Gonga raised their heads. The red-scaled merchant had a raw bass hanging from his toothy snout.

"What now?" He asked.

"No, I mean, you know—*normal* alligators."

Tumbo swallowed the fish without chewing. "What's that supposed to mean?"

Aria's face was bright red again. "No, no. Not that you're not normal, I only meant that—"

"Your skin has changed colors," Gonga droned.

The druidess locked eyes with the dwarf, desperate to change the subject. "Hydras, too," she said matter-of-factly.

Umrick pried another lump of dirt from his armor and peered into the night.

"Hydras, huh?"

"I wouldn't worry about them, though," Aria said. "Ambush predators. If one wanted to come, they'd wait until tonight, long after we've dozed off."

She shot a playful smile toward the dwarf, tossing back another handful of berries from her pocket. Umrick didn't laugh.

"Hilarious," he said.

Before long, the stew was finished, and they had each had their fill of potatoes and crawfish. Conversation during the meal was sparse, and despite Aria's attempt at a joke regarding the hydra, a stiffness had crept its way into the camp. They spent the next few hours half-listening to each others' stories, stealing glances into the darkness, and tensing at every splash and hoot beyond the light.

Before bed, the party sat listening to the symphony of the swamp. It was easy to get lost in the hum of familiar sounds, and it helped distract them from the occasional aberrant notes that made their jaws tighten.

"What do you think they're saying?" Adelphi asked, breaking the relative silence.

"Who?" Umrick asked.

"The animals. The bugs. What do you suppose they're talking about?"

"We could find out," Aria suggested. She sat up on her log and tied her long black curls into a bun.

This caught the others' attention, and they rose to watch as the druidess crossed her legs and took a meditative stance. She closed her eyes, turned her palms skyward, and placed the tips of her middle fingers against her thumbs.

In the darkness, Aria was plunged into the swelling sounds of the Moonmire—thousands upon thousands of buzzes, and hums, and chirps, and growls, and squawks, and gulps. The crackle of the fire disappeared beneath the chorus as she focused, both her ears twitching. She craned her neck to listen for the individual voices, and, slowly, the tones of animals and insects began to fade.

Buzzes turned to bellows. Howls became hollers. Caws slipped into conversation. It was a common tongue, a language she recognized as her own.

The hoot of a nearby owl fell into a deep, resonating

voice. "Where?" It called. "Where? Where has that mouse run off to?"

A lone cricket on the bench beside her was chirping away. The grinding whir of its hind legs became a high-pitched squeal of delight.

"Another night, another song!" It said. "Doing great, everybody! Keep it up! Just nine hours left!"

A soft smile tugged at the edges of Aria's lips. It had been months since she'd taken the time to listen to the sounds of the forest and longer still since she truly heard them.

"Well?" Adelphi asked. "What are they saying?"

"Oh, it's mostly nonsense," Aria said. "Talks of hunting and singing."

Then, another voice—a gruff, throaty one that grunted rhythmically in the dark. A frog, no doubt.

"Man," it groaned.

"Man," another replied.

Aria tried to tune out the other sounds to listen closer to the patch of nearby lily pads.

"There's a man," said a third.

"Man in the water."

"Man in the water."

"Man in the water."

"Man in the water."

Aria's eyes shot open. She lunged for her staff and gazed into the night beyond the colony of frogs. Umrick and the others rose along with her. The dwarf nocked an arrow and flanked out to the left as the rest of the party formed a semi-circle around the campfire.

"What's wrong? Is it a hydra?" The dwarf asked.

"You'd think we would've heard it if it was a hydra," Adelphi said. A nervous laugh came after. "I mean, right?"

"They are stealthy for their size," droned Tumbo.

His red-scaled hands hovered just above a drum strapped to his waist. Adelphi shot him a look that said, "How is that going to help, exactly?" Tumbo didn't seem to notice. Gonga hoisted one of the boat oars up toward his snout and began slowly creeping back toward the raft.

"The frogs," Aria said, straining her eyes in the low light. "They said they saw a man. In the water."

The darkness of the Moonmire was famously dense, but the full summer moon was beaming down that night. In the shimmering ripples, Aria could just make out the beginnings of a shape inching its way toward them. The frogs continued their chant, and before long, the other creatures of the swamp joined in. Their voices boomed in a single pulsing chorus.

Man in the water.

Something labored its way out of the darkness. The shadowy tendrils of the bog clung to its outline, as if begging it to stay—to avoid the light. As it lumbered closer, Aria saw that the voices were right.

It was a man—an ancient one—wading chest-deep through the mire. His long, silvery beard floated atop the water as he hobbled forward, inching himself toward the little island with the help of a walking stick. He wore an oversized sunhat (one with an eagle feather and a tall, crooked top) that covered much of his face, and his simple blue robes were nearly blackened by the muck.

The party stood above the water, stiff as a taut bow. As the man neared the island's edge, Adelphi shot forward to meet him, staff aimed right at his chest.

"That's close enough," she said.

"Oh? Hm?" The man's shoulders jumped. He fumbled with his hat, pushing it back to get a better look at where the voice came from. "Oh! Seems I've made it, then. Hello. Hello there. Yes. Hello."

The flickering fire just reached the man's face, revealing rows of tan wrinkles and eyebrows as thick as ivy. His mouth was entirely covered by a thick, steel-colored mustache that wiggled when he spoke, but judging by the shape of his eyes, he was smiling with all his teeth showing. He placed a pruney hand against his belly and let out a tired chuckle.

"Good to see you. Yes, good indeed. Saw the fire off in the distance, you know. Very good to see you."

Umrick pulled his bow a little tighter, and Aria adjusted her grip on the ancient staff between her fingers. Even Tumbo lifted his palms a bit higher above his drum, ready to strike (for whatever that was worth).

"Who are you?" Adelphi asked, though it sounded more like a demand.

The old man pulled his soaking robe away from his chest.

"Right, right. Look, if you don't mind, I'd love to at least get out of the water here. If you're going to kill me, the least you could do is let me die on dry land." He leaned around Adelphi to get a better look at the muddy mound. "Well, mostly dry, anyway."

Adelphi looked toward the others and gave a half shrug that said, "What am I supposed to do here?" Aria shrugged back, but Umrick didn't take his focus off the stranger.

"Fine," the dwarf said. "But any sudden movements and—"

"Yes, yes. Certain death and all that. Now then..."

The old man trudged out of the water with a splash, struggling his way up the bank and moaning and groaning with each labored step. When he got to the top, he didn't stop. Ignoring the calls of protest behind him, he marched right on over to the fire and plopped down on one of the logs. He then removed his water-filled boots, shook them out, and hung them above the fire to dry.

The party wasn't far behind, and they surrounded the stranger, weapons trained on him from every direction.

"Oh, come now. That's quite enough, isn't it?" He asked.

"Forgive us if we seem suspicious," Aria said.

Umrick huffed. "I couldn't care less if he forgives us or not."

"It's not every day you see an old stranger emerge from the swamp in the dead of night," the druidess continued. "Much less one that takes a seat by your fire uninvited."

"I suppose you're right," the man nodded deeply. "But then again, if I were here to kill you, would I have removed my *shoes*?"

He lifted one leg and wiggled his mud-covered toes.

Gonga blinked sideways. "I... do not see what that has to do with this."

"Hard to commit murder when your feet are all

muddy," the stranger explained. "Leaves footprints, you know. I think that's one of the first things they teach you in... murdering school?"

At this, the party lowered their guard for the first time, disarmed by the stupidity of it all.

"Who are you, old man?" Umrick asked.

"Ah, yes. Forgot that part. Sorry. The name's Caldur Cobris—traveling wizard."

At that, the old man tossed his hands up to the side and shot a flaccid stream of sizzling fireworks from his fingertips, first to the left, then to the right. The dancing lights flashed against the trees, illuminating shapes in the distance which scurried back toward the cover of darkness.

"Pretty cool, huh?" He asked, pleased with himself. "Wizard! Say, do you mind if I get some of... whatever's in that pot? Haven't eaten in days, you know."

Adelphi was stone-faced. "No."

"No, you don't mind, or no, I can't have any?" He smiled up at her.

She smacked her palm against her forehead and forced a long sigh through her nose.

"The first. Fine."

Caldur certainly ate like he hadn't in days. After his fourth bowl, he finally sat back against the log and patted his belly, lifting his muddy feet up to the fire.

"That was a fine meal. A fine meal. Thank you," he said.

"I don't mean to pry, but who are you again? How did you get here?" Aria asked.

For the next twenty minutes or so, Caldur told them (in excruciating detail) his story about traveling into the

Moonmire in search of a remote lizard village. He got lost, of course, and had been trying to find his way out of the swamp for nearly a week. The story was a simple one, but Caldur found ways to make it last much longer than necessary, going off on tangents, interjecting unrelated stories about his youth, and providing all the context for how he knew the names of certain trees throughout the bog. By the end of it, Aria was almost certain the man wasn't there to kill them, and if he were, she wished he would get on with it already.

Just as Caldur was heading down another rabbit hole toward the end of his tale, Aria caught a glimpse of something peculiar. It was a small blue jay, resting happily upon a twisted tree branch high above Caldur's head. It shoved its tiny face into its sapphire plumage, rifled around for a bit, then flitted down to rest on the old man's shoulder.

"Oh my," he said, scratching at the bird's chest with a crooked finger. "Hello. Yes, hello there. Anyway, where was I? Ah, yes, that business with the boa constrictor."

With that, Caldur continued spinning his story, paying the little blue thing on his shoulder no mind. The bird, however, never took its eyes off him. Aria watched it carefully, studying its features and observing the way it seemed to hang on Caldur's every word. The magic of her spell had not yet worn off, so she scooted a bit closer and whispered in its direction.

"Hey. Can you understand me?" Her voice trickled out as a soft whistle.

The blue jay's head whipped to the left and locked her

in an intense stare. After a moment, it gave a single, careful nod.

"Do you know this man?" Aria asked.

The songbird looked back at Caldur. Its head twitched left and right, but after a moment, it turned back and nodded once more.

"Is he dangerous?"

At this, the little blue bird stared at the ground. It seemed to be awfully deep in thought or hesitating—Aria couldn't tell which. Just before she moved to ask a different question, the blue jay spoke.

"Yes."

Its voice was deep, far deeper than she had braced for, and its tenor carried with it a certain wisdom that far exceeded that of an ordinary songbird.

A wave of chills crawled up the back of the druidess's neck like a skeletal hand. It was the same feeling that always washed over her in the presence of danger—*real* danger. She watched Caldur carefully as he waved his hands back and forth, laughed with his belly, and made a funny voice for one of the characters in his story. The sound was muffled and distant over the rush of blood in her ears. She inched her fingertips closer to her staff, but just as they touched it, the blue jay spoke again.

"Then again, so are you."

Before she could ask what the bird meant, a chilling screech echoed through the swamp, silencing the thousands of tiny voices in the darkness. There was splashing in the distance, but within seconds, it grew into an explosion of water, as if half a dozen bulls were stampeding through the muck toward them.

The party shot up and lunged for their weapons, and Caldur hopped to his feet without putting his boots on.

At the edge of the light, a hulking, wriggling shadow appeared. The black-on-black shape stood nearly as tall as the bone-white trees jutting out of the muck. With a rumbling hiss, a single, scaly head with glassy black eyes wormed its way out of the shadows. Its serpent-like mouth opened to reveal shiny rows of tightly packed fangs as another viperish head appeared. Then another. And another. And another.

Umrick's voice crept like ice over Aria's shoulder. "You've got to be kidding me."

From beyond the wall of darkness, a hydra writhed and plodded its way through the mire toward them, five sets of jaws dripping ichor and venom into the inky waters below. Each of its many sets of eyes was trained on a different target—a different meal—and the muscles beneath its leathery hide rippled with each heavy step.

"Don't worry! Don't you worry! Traveling wizard coming through." Caldur wrestled past Aria and shuffled barefoot toward the edge of the island. "I've got this one. I can do it. I got it. Okay. Here we go."

Before the others could protest, Caldur smacked his still-pruney hands together as if he were trying to start a friction fire. Then, he took a half-crouched stance and turned his fingers toward the creature.

"Hey! You!" He shouted in a tinny voice. "Git!"

With that, a shower of harmless fireworks burst from

his hands and trickled into the waters beneath the hydra. It was a sad rainbow of sparkles that could hardly singe the wings of a fly. The hydra's eyes locked on Caldur, and it reared all five of its heads back at once. Aria braced herself.

"So this is how the old man dies," she thought.

But Caldur didn't die. With a violent screech, the hydra scrambled away from the sparks. It hissed and kicked, flipping over itself before tearing off into the darkness of the Moonmire.

As the sound of snapping trees and heavy steps faded into the night, the choir of crickets resumed their song, and Caldur dispelled the shimmering stream of sparkles. Then he turned with a grin and gave the party a crooked thumbs up.

There were many questions after that, most of which Caldur answered with, "I told you—wizard!" Then he'd let out a wheezy laugh and ask if they'd like to hear another story. They did not, of course. They were far more interested in *this* story, but that did very little in the way of discouraging him.

Not long after, Caldur Cobris was gone. He declined to tag along with the others to Tumbo's village, choosing instead to brave the shadows of the Moonmire on his own. After all, he knew the way out now, and he'd be back on dry land within a day or two. Reluctantly, the party agreed to see him off, and they shared what little provisions they had to ensure his journey was as safe as it could be.

In the crackling firelight, the party watched the old man slip back into the muck and disappear into the darkness. As the others returned to their cots and logs, Aria hung back, watching as the little blue jay preened itself in the tree limbs above.

It was a strange night. No one would argue that, but the druidess had the sneaking suspicion that there was more to the story than any of them could know. She wondered what would've happened had Caldur not shown up. She wondered about the blue jay. She wondered if she'd be stuck wondering, or if they'd meet the traveling wizard again someday, perhaps somewhere dryer and with fewer hydras. She wondered what stories he would tell then and if she'd be more inclined to listen to them.

As Caldur's outline finally vanished, the little blue bird flitted away with him, and Aria was left alone at the edge of the island. A monotonous voice called out to her from nearby. It was Gonga. He stood only a few feet away with his oar resting against his shoulder, staring with a blank expression into the darkness. Aria wondered how long he'd been standing there.

"I told you."

"Told me what?" She asked.

"That a fire will keep the biting things away."

SMALL VICTORIES

L avender sank her fingernails into the railing of
the Iron Harpy, her face as green as the seafoam
clinging to the wet wooden hull. The waves of
nausea started in her toes, working their way up past the
back of her knees, twisting her stomach into knots. Her
neck felt hot and numb, and her chin quivered with each
rise and fall of the ship.

With her mouth in an O shape, she exhaled slowly,
then pulled the briny sea air in through her nose. For the
first time in two weeks, she managed to keep her breakfast
where it was meant to be. It was a small victory, and she
hardly felt like celebrating, but it *was* a victory. Her throat

was scratchy and raw from the constant sickness, and she was grateful, for once, that nausea was the worst of it.

"Finally found our sea legs, have we?" A familiar, dry voice called from behind her.

Lavender turned, slow as a glacier. Any sudden movement might flip her stomach and send her lunging for the railing again. Barnabus stood just a few feet away, leaning against a gnarled staff. His ashen beard whipped in the ocean wind, and he was wearing a sympathetic smile.

The halfling girl nodded gingerly behind a curly curtain of golden locks as the ship dipped down in the swell and a white mist sprayed over the bow. The acid splashed in her belly.

"Too bad we're... only a few days from port."

Barnabus peered out toward the horizon and laughed. It was a genuine laugh, the kind that came from the belly. Beneath the wide brim of his hat, Lavender could see the wizard had caught some sun on this little excursion. The wrinkles around his face had deepened to a bronzy hue, and his eyes seemed bluer and brighter than ever before.

"Well," he said, "Better late than never I sup—"

If Barnabus finished his sentence, Lavender didn't hear it. A cacophony of crashing water and creaking wood erupted from the front of the ship. The ocean swelled into a dome, pressing up from the surface and lifting the front of the Iron Harpy skyward. The vessel lurched back, creaking and moaning, as something enormous rose from the deep.

Lavender shot for the railing, wrapped her arm around it, and squeezed with all her might. With her other hand, she wrestled the short bow off her back. Barnabus did not lunge for the railing. In fact, he hardly seemed bothered by the excitement at all.

The old man tapped his staff against the deck—two quick knocks—and remained right where he was. Even as the ship reached its highest point, Barnabus did not move. The wizard stuck straight out from the deck, as if gravity were an optional thing, and his iron hair fell from his shoulders in ringlets toward the angry sea beneath him.

Lavender paid little attention to the old man. She was far too busy clinging on for dear life. She shoved her foot into the posts of the railing as the ship went vertical, and as it crashed back down, she leapt away and rolled along the planks. Her eyes darted all around, glancing past the towering masts and over the rusty cannons, waiting for the creature to show itself.

It was a sea monster—she was certain of that. She expected to see wriggling tentacles creep over the rails, their suction cups tensing and feeling the air, dripping a sticky ichor onto the lacquered floor. What she did not expect was what actually appeared.

In a pillar of brine and foam, a human-like creature burst from the ocean—so impossibly large that the sun disappeared behind his back, bathing the deck in midday twilight. Even waist-deep in the sea, the blue-skinned titan stood as tall as the ship's highest mast.

His thick, pearly beard dumped gallons of water (and a few very confused fish) onto the deck as he swung around and planted a wagon-sized hand onto the planks. The Iron Harpy sank and rocked beneath its weight, instantly pinned in place like a dried butterfly on a corkboard.

The giant took his time then. He studied each of the soaked and prone creatures before him, including Lavender, with a pair of massive violet eyes. He wore a vacant, almost bored expression—the kind of emotionless stoicism one might expect of a tyrant. She felt like an ant beneath a magnifying glass on a sunny day, and the little bow in her hand had never felt so small.

"Well," said the giant, "If it isn't *small folk*."

He seemed to be speaking softly, but the voice rumbled from his throat like an approaching thunderstorm.

"You do not belong here."

The titan spoke each word with a space in between so there could be no misunderstanding. The crew was silent. A few sailors glanced at the cannons with wide, hungry eyes, then up to the wizard, who, almost imperceptibly, shook his head. The others were either too stunned or too smart to do anything at all.

"These waters," said the giant, "*My* waters—are forbidden to *your kind*."

The words dripped with venom. His gaze crawled and lingered over each of them like a spider wrapping its prey, assessing them, *judging* them.

"Then again," he continued, "You are stupid. And small. You cannot be blamed for this. It is your nature, after all. I should expect no different." His grip on the deck tightened then, and a board snapped under the pressure of his colossal index finger. "As king, it is my right to sentence you to death, but I am not so heartless. I will give you a chance—a *single* chance—to stay my hand. Give me *one good reason* why I should not sink this ship and drag each of you into the depths, gasping and kicking—powerless as you are."

The whole crew then turned to the wizard, and Lavender joined them. The old man nodded in the shade of his hat, peering at the salty puddles around his feet. He then tapped his staff once more and took a single step forward.

"Just and powerful king," Barnabus said with as much reverence as his wizened voice could muster, "Surely, we mean no offense. We are unwise to the laws and treaties that govern these waters. Stupid, as you say. For that, you have our sincerest apologies." He gave a slight bow. "My companions and I carry an urgent message to the capital city of Alabaster. There is a storm coming."

At this, the giant furrowed his brow and looked toward the horizon.

"Not one of lightning and thunder, my lord," continued Barnabus, "But of blood and fire. A conflict, one which looms ever closer, even as we now speak. It will not be bound by land or borders or laws or treaties. It will spread, even here—a blight and a shadow. I fear you will find it far less willing to parlay than us small folk."

The titan returned his gaze to the wizard with the same bored expression.

"But all is not lost, oh King of the Deep. Our message may yet dispel the storm before it can swell," Barnabus said. Then he paused and considered his next words. "We would not dare to knowingly trespass. Surely, in your infinite wisdom, you know this to be true. We ask for your forgiveness and for your grace so that we may pass and complete our quest. It could mean the difference between life and death, both for our kind, and for yours, and for all."

The giant was a statue, huge and still and unreadable. The sails flapped in the ocean breeze. A single seagull squawked as it fluttered down and found a sunny spot on the giant's knuckle. The waves crashed against the hull.

The giant's deep-blue nostrils flared as he released a long, steady sigh through his nose. A gust of wind came with it, hot and stinking of the ocean. Lavender's hair whipped against her shoulders.

The giant then stood to his full height, towering above the Iron Harpy like a storm cloud. With the sun behind his head, his violet eyes glowed like a dying star—one lashing out in a final, brilliant display of light and fury.

"You must have misheard me, *wizard*," he growled.

The sky changed then, as quick as a match strike. Roiling charcoal clouds rumbled into existence above the giant's head, swallowing the brilliant blue sky and plunging the surrounding sea into shadow.

The calm waters grew restless. Rain fell in sheets. The tide shoved against the hull, as if urging the ship to leave, and all the color of the world drained away beneath the overcast—all except for the titan's burning gaze.

Then a flash. Thunder cracked with a sharp shattering sound, and a sizzling bolt of lashing electricity burst into the giant's palm. He gripped it like a blade. The white-hot arcs danced across the skin of his forearm, stretching out like witch's fingers toward his shoulder. The lightning flickered in his eyes.

"I asked for a *good* reason."

There was a stillness then. A single heartbeat when all the fear was forgotten—when terror gave way to awe and wonder. And then it was gone.

Barnabus shot out a hand toward Lavender, and a wave of force sent her sliding across the deck—away from him. The titan hurled the lightning down at the wizard, whose open palm was still outstretched toward the halfling. The old man was smiling.

It was a soft expression.

It was the kind that said, "Sorry about that, little one."

The bolt exploded into the deck like grapeshot. In a cloud of smoke and splinters, Barnabus vanished. The lightning tore a hole straight through the ship—a jagged, gaping wound filled with darkness and gushing water.

Some crewmates launched themselves from the deck into the freezing waves below. Some climbed the riggings or scurried below deck, and some launched harpoons at the giant's belly. They tapped against his ancient armor and fell harmlessly into the churning waves.

Others scrambled for the cannons, shouting orders and wailing into the storm. They fumbled with the main guns, packing them with shaking hands before lighting the fuses and firing. Most missed.

The giant roared, a thunderous sound that shook the ship itself, and swung a mighty hand across the sky. The tallest mast cracked like a twig beneath the force, and the top half came tumbling down with a sickening crunch.

Lavender darted for the upper deck and dove toward the stairs as another blast of splintery shrapnel erupted behind her. She clambered up the steps and took cover behind the captain's wheel, then popped out and loosed two arrows toward the giant's neck. Between the smoke and rain, she couldn't even see where they landed.

She fired a third and a fourth, feeling stupid and small and furious, then took cover again. The ship was sinking, Barnabus was gone, and she had a bow the size of a giant's littlest eyelash.

She was going to die here, and she knew that. Lavender always assumed she'd be terrified at this moment. When there were no options left. When no help was coming. When it finally sank in that there was nothing she could do. Nothing at all.

And she *should* have been scared. Her chest should have felt like the deck of the ship, a jagged hole filled with darkness. She should have been destroyed by the loss of the wizard. She should have been torn to pieces, hiding in a corner, weeping and babbling about how she didn't want to die—not here. Not now.

But Lavender didn't feel much of anything at all. Just a dull rage that felt more like frustration than anything else. Her face was hot. Her hands were shaking. Her jaw was tight.

At that moment, when she should have been drowning in despair, all she wanted to do was fire arrows until she didn't have any left. She could drown later. So that's what she did.

Ten arrows left.

This is a stupid way to die.

Seven.

You were supposed to be this powerful thing—this incredible magic man. And you left. You died.

Four.

What was the point of all this, then? We just lose? That's it? Heroes win, old man. We were supposed to win.

Two.

This is a stupid way to die.

One.

Lavender pulled her final arrow back and bared her teeth. This one was going for its eye. She would hold it as long as she needed to. This one was for the wizard. This one was for *her*.

Another round of cannon fire. The giant disappeared in a cloud of dust and gunpowder smoke. When the wind tore the cover away, the titan was holding his enormous hands above his head, and another bolt of lightning slammed into his open palms. This time the flickering sparks formed a thick, crackling maul of white-hot fire. With a final roar, he swung the hammer of lightning down into the center of the ship.

Lavender held her breath. With the bowstring tucked against her cheek and her hands as still as stones, she waited. The giant's arms swung down. His shoulders followed. His head came with it, all gnashing teeth and violet eyes. As the maul sank into the planks, she opened her fingers. The deck exploded in a violent burst of wood and light, fire and lightning.

· · ·

The next thing Lavender knew, she was cold. Very cold. It was dark here, wherever she was. What had she been doing before everything was dark and cold? She couldn't quite remember. It seemed important, whatever it was. The thought slipped through her mind like fog between a child's fingers.

Her vision came in blurry flashes. There were bubbles. They rose past her face, catching what little light there was before lazily floating away. They were pretty, she thought. She wished there were more of them.

Now there was a soft blue light, the cold kind. The color of ice. Had it always been there? Everything was so quiet. Muted. Gentle. She felt like she was floating. Totally weightless. It would've been nice if it weren't for the cold. The taste of salt filled her mouth, her nose. Her head was pounding, she realized, a steady thrum from back to front. Why was it so cold?

Now there was a different light above her. Brighter. Smaller. Maybe it would be warm up there. She thought about kicking, about flapping her arms, but everything felt numb and slow. She wasn't sure if she was moving or not.

Light and sound rushed into the world as Lavender's head burst from the water. She choked down a chest-full of air, and it burned like fire behind her ribs. Her arms shot for a hunk of the ship's deck, and she wrapped herself around it, head spinning, bobbing up and down in the freezing water.

Her vision was still blurry, but she could see it—the giant—standing waist-deep in the sea, looming proudly over the wreckage like a hunter above its prey. It had one eye closed, but the other stared down at her above a flat, triumphant smile. The Iron Harpy was split in two, each smoldering half slowly sinking into a ring of bubbles and debris. But there was something else there.

It was a figure—shimmering like rubies in the lightning light. He was standing on a crate, floating there in the water, wearing a wide-brimmed hat. He looked like he'd gotten too much sun.

"Bar... nabus?" Lavender whispered, then coughed up a mess of seawater.

She couldn't see his face clearly, but she saw his beard twitch. He might have been smiling.

"Sorry about that, little one. Went a bit deeper than expected."

Barnabus peered up at the titan as claws of electricity raked the sky behind him.

"We would have passed peacefully, you know?" The wizard called over the roar of fire and wind and thunder. "But look at all this. You've gone and hurt my little friend here—all these other people as well. I'm afraid I can't forgive that."

A voice like a thunderclap erupted overhead. "You'll die with them, *wizard*!"

The giant reached down with a colossal hand and snapped off the splintered remains of the ship's tallest mast. Then, with all the fury of a hurricane, he hurled the jagged shard at Barnabus. It pierced the air like a javelin, punching a hole in the rain and smoke with a deafening crack. The water bent beneath its speed.

Barnabus flicked his staff in a small circle, and a shim-

mering green portal swirled into existence at the edge of
his hat. The mast disappeared through the vortex, and
Barnabus jerked the staff once again. The hole in space
winked shut.

"*What?*" Roared the giant.

A heartbeat later, a second portal opened. This one just
behind the giant's back. A streak of black came hurtling
out.

Then there was a wet sucking sound, and the splintered mast pierced the giant's heart from behind.

Lavender watched as the titan stumbled forward,
clutching the bloody stake in his chest, tugging and
pushing at it in vain. He stepped back, staggered, then fell.
The sea rolled beneath him like dark blue bed sheets.

The roiling charcoal clouds thinned, burning away
beneath the noonday sun. With a squawk, the same
seagull landed on the giant's still kneecap, bobbing gently
in the calm water and preening itself in the sunshine.

"All right then, are we?" Barnabus asked.

Lavender pulled herself from the sea with a grunt and a
moan. She sat cross-legged on her hunk of driftwood, and
her hair fell around her face, dripping saltwater and blood
into the waves beneath her. She was cold, and she was
soaked to the bone, and her head was throbbing more than
it ever had in her life.

But she wasn't the least bit seasick—and that was
more than a small victory.

S oft orange light trickled in through the stone
window on the left side of the chamber. The
ambient glow of a dozen torches at the base of the
tower wasn't enough to see by, but it was enough to cast
shadows, to create shapes in the darkness, and to give the
vaguest impression of domed ceilings somewhere overhead. There was a dresser and a chest, a single chair and a
vanity, and at the back of the room, a lavish four-poster
bed draped in a hundred shades of black—a wide square
bathed in layers of grim velvet.

There, trembling in the darkness, was a dwarf
clutching his soaked-through sheets with all his fingers.
Daggur's wringing-wet hair framed his face in sticky
strands as a single bead of sweat fell from his nose and
disappeared into the dark sheets. The thick braids that
clung to his cheeks and chin were crusted in hours-old
drool, and his mustache stuck out in all the wrong places.
He must've been thrashing again.

If someone had entered the room just then, if they'd
discovered him there, unable to steady his breath, glazed
in a cold sweat, staring wide-eyed at the shapes in the
dark, they wouldn't have believed it.

Daggur wasn't the type to have nightmares. He was a
knight—a soldier. He slept when he was tired, he awoke
when it was time, and little else of interest happened

between the two. Even now, years after earning his position as captain of the royal guard, long after his first night
feeling awkward and uncomfortable in this opulent chamber, sleep remained a utilitarian practice. Dreaming was a
luxury, one he rarely had time to enjoy.

But that was before. Before the orcs arrived. Before the
talks of peace and treaties. Before the worm. Before the
failure. Now, a single dream plagued the dwarf, repeating
endlessly each time he closed his eyes.

Daggur stood in the center of a dark stone street
somewhere on the eastern side of the city under the mountain. Drenched in torchlight, he looked first to his left, then
to his right. He had the nagging feeling that he should
recognize more, that the place should be familiar, but the
details were all wrong. The dwarven structures around him
rose toward the rocky ceiling overhead at impossible
angles, shop signs were written in strange characters that
he couldn't understand, and there were people—so many
people—all running.

There were dwarves in heavy armor—soldiers, he
thought—sprinting to the east and shouting unintelligible
orders. Citizens flooded past to the west, dwarves and
humans and other folks. All of their faces were missing.
Daggur watched the people blur past in both directions,
wondering which way he was meant to go.

Then he heard it—that sound. That deep, deafening
rumble, like a thousand minecarts rolling toward him. The
sound of the city crumbling. The sound of thousands Of

years of dwarven history being erased—being devoured. The sound of the deepworm.

Daggur stumbled toward the noise, following the swelling river of faceless soldiers. Then he blinked, and when his eyes reopened, he was standing shoulder to shoulder with the royal guard, watching as the colossal worm writhed its way through the streets. Its blubbery underbelly undulated with sickening efficiency, propelling it overtop storefronts and through ancient libraries, swallowing entire structures with its gaping maw and flattening others as it passed.

Daggur watched the soldiers move into strategic positions around him. Some gathered on rooftops. Others stood sideways on nearby buildings. Some floated overhead. A pair of dwarves draped in brightly colored linens rode sidesaddle atop a massive butterfly that flitted above the city. The insect trilled like a dolphin (it didn't seem so strange in the moment).

Squads of dwarves launched javelins into the rubbery hide along the worm's side. Ballista bolts whistled through the air and exploded against the crusty scales along the beast's back. One dwarf with a miniature catapult was busy instructing a group of goblins to sit in the bucket. He handed each of them a bomb and a pair of aviator's goggles and sent them careening toward the destruction.

The worm seemed entirely unaware of the resistance. It just ate, mindlessly slinking its way along, swallowing homes and schools and government buildings without prejudice or concern for who might be inside.

But as it passed, as it crunched its way through

markets and neighborhoods, nothing was left in its path. There was no rubble. There were no signs of devastation. There was *nothing*. Just a deep, endless blackness where the city used to be, like the night sky without a speck of starlight. The capital was mostly darkness now.

Then Daggur was alone. Only the one street remained, surrounded entirely by the void. Up ahead, a single dwarf in gleaming golden armor stood with his back to the captain, a rusty hammer dangling by his side.

Daggur narrowed his eyes. "King Andor?"

The figure turned. Not enough to look at him, but enough to acknowledge the sound. Daggur blinked, and when his eyes reopened, the worm was there with its titanic mouth wreathed around the king, tensing and excreting thick strands of umber goo. It was happening in slow motion.

Daggur's hand shot out. He tried to dash forward, but his feet were fused to the stone beneath him, melding into the street up to the ankles. He screamed, tugging at his legs and gnashing his teeth with the effort. Then his teeth fell out, and everything sped up.

The deepworm crashed into the king. He was swallowed in an instant, along with the street beneath him. The next moment, so was Daggur.

It was dark inside the worm. The air was hot and sticky, but the captain felt nothing beneath him, as if he were floating in the void itself. Just endless black and moist air.

"We lost," a puff of hot air spoke in his ear. It was the king's voice. "And where were you?"

Then there was another sound, a sickening crunch and a gush of unseen liquid. A sliver of light appeared in the darkness, and two hands gripped its sides. They pried open the slit, and a strange pale light seeped into the space. A face followed after.

It was an orc. Their tusks glittered in the dim. They reached a hand inside the void, grunting with the effort, but as Daggur reached toward it, another shape passed in front of him. It was the king. His armor was dripping with ichor, and his right leg was missing. They grabbed ahold of one another, and the orc dragged the king out through the sliver of light. As his one boot passed the threshold, the tear in the void sealed shut, and Daggur was left alone in the nothingness.

That's when he woke up. Just as the sliver closed, just as the darkness washed over him, Daggur jolted awake, soaked in sweat, gripping his sheets like a child, but there were no parents nearby to scream for.

With a bang, the door to Daggur's chamber slammed open, and flickering torchlight spilled inside. A soldier that the captain didn't recognize entered.

"Sir?" They called.

Daggur released his sheets. "What is it?" His voice was thin and awkward.

The soldier's wide eyes darted around the dark room. His lips opened and shut silently, as if he couldn't find the right phrase.

"The king. He's gone. He's just... *gone*."

. . .

Daggur flew through the city like a raven from a lightning storm. He clambered down winding staircases and through half-lit alleyways, across quiet squares and past vacant market stalls. His boots slapped against the damp stone, a frantic beat that only just outpaced the thumping behind his breastplate.

It had been three weeks since the deepworm razed the east side of the capital; three weeks since the dwarves and orcs stood together against the destruction; three weeks since the king was devoured; and three weeks since his body was pried from its belly, still breathing but changed.

Now the king was gone. Daggur was supposed to be there—to keep him safe—and where was he? Panting in the dark, too scared to leave his bed? A cold sweat collected at the back of his neck, and with each heavy breath, a new, horrible vision of what may have befallen the king flashed across his mind. The others were mobilizing now, crawling the city in squads, preparing to sound the alarms. He couldn't wait for that.

The dwarven knight flew from another alley and skidded to a halt in a night-drenched courtyard near the city center. His insides twisted into a knot—one pulled tight by pity and shame and gratitude.

King Andor stood propped on a wooden crutch beneath the shadow of a towering statue, still as the city itself. He was wrapped in a simple nightgown, his auburn curls pulled back and his beard unbrushed. He was alive.

For a moment, Daggur felt as if his feet were fused to

the cobblestones beneath him. He stared at the king's back, picturing the lamprey-like mouth of the deepworm encircling his form. Then he blinked, and the king was still there, staring up at the stone figure. Daggur trotted toward him.

"Sir?"

King Andor turned. Not enough to look at him, but enough to acknowledge the sound. He was different now, Daggur thought. It wasn't the bandaged stump beneath his right knee or the silvery scar that crawled its way from his neck to his cheek, either. It wasn't the unwashed hair or the lack of shimmering armor. It was something else.

The king gazed at the statue of the ferocious orc warrior in the center of the square. It was Thrag, the only non-dwarf to ever be immortalized in the capital under the mountain—the same orc from Daggur's dream.

A long silence passed between the two dwarves.

"He saved my life," said the king.

"Yes, sir."

A pause.

"Not a dwarf?"

Daggur's eyes fell to the cobblestones. He chewed the inside of his lip, then lifted his chin to stare into Thrag's perfectly carved face.

"No, sir."

"An orc."

"Yes, sir."

"Hm."

Another silence.

"A thousand years of war," said the king. "And all it took to end it was the loss of a leg."

Daggur said nothing.

"Seems like a small price to pay. Wouldn't you say?"

"It's not my place, sir."

"And if it were? Speak your mind."

Daggur swallowed a wad of something.

"It was a rather large leg for a dwarf, sir."

Neither laughed. Both smiled.

"I wish you hadn't had to pay it."

"But it is paid," said Andor.

The captain remained silent.

"Would you have paid it?" Asked the king.

Daggur studied the cobbles through the vacant space beneath the king's right knee.

"Gladly, sir."

"A thousand years..." The king's voice was little more than a push of air. "All this time... We were wrong, weren't we?"

Daggur lifted his eyes to the orc. Thrag seemed to stare back.

"Yes, sir."

Then a deeper hush fell over the square, and the two dwarves stood shoulder to shoulder, thinking of blood and stone and debts and forgiveness.

THE BITS IN BETWEEN

everal missed his bed. He longed for the crisp, familiar embrace of fresh cotton sheets, the weight of a hand-stitched quilt, the cool side of a downy pillow.

He missed rising in the early mornings when he would step out into the damp before dawn to listen as the world sang itself awake. The steam from his coffee cup would drift over the backside of his hand to float above the dewdrops on the grass, wafting and flitting in the low light before finding its way into the fog that hung low over the hills. It was those quiet moments that tugged at his heart, those few precious minutes just before the sun edged its way into view to wish him a good day. He hardly remembered the warmth of its greeting at all.

In truth, there were a great many things Ceveral had taken for granted. The abundance of clean clothes hanging neatly in his closet. The privacy of a bathroom with a door. The convenience of a three-minute walk to the shop, where there was food and plenty of it.

He even found himself longing for things he might have considered inconveniences before he knew any better. Things like polishing the floors in his home. Pulling weeds from his garden. Finding time in his schedule for a haircut every few months. They felt like distant dreams—foreign and quaint and perfect.

Once again, Ceveral was lying awake, somewhere miles below the surface, thinking of home. His top half was wrapped in a too-small, scratchy blanket, and the oozy bedrock beneath him dug into his back like knuckles. No matter how he shifted and squirmed, there was no comfort to be found.

These were the parts of adventuring that no one ever spoke about—the bits in between that were notably absent from every bard song, every legend, and every folktale.

Ceveral sighed, a soft sound that echoed against the cavern walls, and took to counting the stalactites looming overhead. They looked like teeth, he thought—a thousand dripping fangs waiting to swallow him whole. Another bead of water tapped him on the forehead and trickled into his soaking hairline to join the others. He rolled over for the fifth time, found the driest stone he could, and planted his shock of bright-orange curls against it.

The others seemed to be sleeping soundly enough. In the low green glow of the brightshrooms, he watched their shoulders rise and fall in slow, rhythmic patterns. Lucky them.

Some nights, he lay there waiting for one of his companions to huff and roll toward him, unable to rest, unable to dream. They would talk, he imagined, about what they missed most from before. What they wanted to do first when they reached the surface again. About the foods they craved. About their families. About how awful their journey so far had been, and about how adventuring was not at all like the stories.

Other times, he imagined one of them jolting awake and tossing their blanket to the side.

"I can't do this anymore," they would say.

"Do what?" Ceveral would ask, wiping his eyes as if he'd been asleep all along. "Is everything alright?"

"No. No, it's not alright. I hate this. All of it."

The others would stir then, fumbling for their weapons in the darkness and searching for the source of the commotion.

"This is miserable," the one would continue. "I just want to go home. Don't you?"

And then the others would grow still. They would sit there in the darkness together, letting the silence do its work. Each of them would find something—a pebble, a mushroom, a shadow—and stare into it, unsure of what to say, unsure if anything needed to be said at all. And there would be some measure of comfort among them—all miserable, but miserable together, at least.

And then another would speak up.

"But if we don't do this, who will?"

The conversation would end after that. Slowly, one after another, each of Ceveral's companions would lie down and stare into the darkness until, hours later, sleep finally washed over them. It wouldn't be much, but somewhere within those eight words, there would be a change. That simple phrase would be enough. Enough to dull the ache in their legs. Enough to dampen the hunger. Enough to remind them of why they were there. Enough to say that, when this was all over, it will have been worth it.

But that never happened.

At the end of each long day, they made camp with what little supplies they had left, held the same argument about whether or not to start a fire, decided against it, and eased down onto the unforgiving rocks in a circle. Within minutes, the others would be snoring softly, and Ceveral would be there, wide awake, staring at the salivating ceiling overhead, having pretend conversations in the dark. Tonight was no different from the rest. Tomorrow would be more of the same.

Nearby, a bit of light glinted off the surface of his well-worn lute. It was glazed in the damp, and the glow of fungi along its body reflected softly against Ceveral's skin like the surface of a moonlit pond. Any day now, the lute's bridge would swell, and its strings would begin to cake with rust.

Instruments like that weren't built for the damp. They

weren't made to be dragged into the darkest reaches of the world. They had no business on any adventures. They weren't cut out for all this. Ceveral caught the vague outline of his reflection in the glimmer. He looked different and small.

At home, insomnia was not an altogether vile thing. On the nights where sleep evaded him, Ceveral traveled down the stairs, careful not to let the floorboards groan too much, and dipped like a shadow into his study. He selected his finest quills, arranged his papers and inks in their ideal locations around the desk by his piano, and began working.

Sometimes he tweaked the harmonies of an existing composition, and other times he would draft something new. He wondered what he would have chosen tonight. Something melodious and soothing, he decided. A lullaby, perhaps.

Maybe he would have chosen the harp instead, plucking ever so quietly as not to wake the ones sleeping overhead. It would take hours, of course, and by the time it was all said and done, he would have composed deep into the night, sacrificing those early morning moments that he cherished so much. The candles around the room would be half melted, his fingers stiff and blistered, and his eyelids drooping like the moon beyond the window. But it would be finished, and he would be glad that the next day held little excitement and that he could spend it at home, surrounded by strings and brass and keys.

But Ceveral wasn't home. And down here, soaked in the dark and damp, he didn't feel much like playing.

The church was on fire. Smoke billowed inside the sanctuary as oily flames crawled up the velvet tapestries lining the walls. Like a thousand red-hot tentacles, the fire licked at the edges of the ancient murals stretching across the domed ceiling, and the portraits winced away from the heat. The paint cracked and withered, peeling free from the plaster beneath and sending heroes and angels alike fleeing for safety high above the church floor. The once heavenly scene contorted into a blackened, misshapen thing—a hellscape within the smoke.

At the front of the chapel, a marble dais stood bathed in firelight and cinders. The two hundred candles which once surrounded the pulpit were now a pool of bubbling wax that dripped in fat globs onto the hot stone below, popping and hissing like a tar pit. All that remained of the holy text upon the altar were two brass buckles amidst a smoldering pile of ash.

Pews snapped and splintered. Iron fixtures burned red and sagged in places. Even the towering stained-glass windows along the walls shattered beneath the swelling heat, sending fragments of saints and goddesses crashing to the floor. And there, in the center of it all, was a single knight lying face down on the carpet.

. . .

Outside, the dark city streets were thrumming with movement. A crowd of townsfolk, many of whom were still wrapped in their nightgowns, gathered on the sidewalk across from the cathedral. Some offered prayers. Others cried quietly. A few simply stared. With the window frames aglow from the fire inside, the chapel seemed to stare back.

Between the crowd and the blaze, two dozen important-looking people in thick red trench coats bustled along the cobblestones. Sigils decorated their chests and shoulders, small shields with the letters AFCU. The Arcane Fire Containment Unit moved in squads of four, barking orders and taking positions around the low stone wall surrounding the courtyard at the front of the church.

"Ready?" An officer shouted.

"Sir!" The others said together.

Then the incantations began. The squads worked in unison, waving their hands in wide circles, reciting a language that few in the crowd could recognize. Glowing arcane seals materialized along the cobbles around each group, and a moment later, columns of water erupted from the streets. The geysers shot over the wall and collided against the cathedral with a hiss, dowsing the ancient stone before spilling into the square.

It was almost dawn now. From the back of the crowd, another figure in red appeared. The end of a cigar hung loosely from his lips as he squirmed his way through the crowd, popped open an umbrella, and crossed the street.

The officer barking orders turned at the man's approach and saluted.

"Captain Ivan!"

The man with the cigar gave a dismissive wave and puffed a cloud of smoke into the air. "What are we looking at, Carver?"

Officer Carver glanced back at the chapel. "Well, it isn't great, sir."

"Unnatural?"

"I'm afraid so, sir. We've been giving it everything we've got, but, well—watch."

Carver tapped one of the mages on the shoulder and directed her toward a shattered window near the front of the cathedral.

"Show him."

The recruit gave a tired nod and aimed her geyser to fire at a hole in the glass where furnace-like flames were still pouring out. The column of water collided with the window with a crunch as steam billowed over the church roof.

"That's enough," Carver said.

The mage twisted the geyser away, but the flames beneath remained. If anything, they seemed fiercer —angrier.

Ivan rubbed the scruff of his chin. "So, water's not working. What are you thinking? Something alchemical?"

"Could be..." Carver swallowed hard. "May I speak freely, sir?"

The grizzled captain blinked slowly and pulled smoke into his mouth.

"I'll take that as a yes." Carver looked over his shoulder at the flames. "Arcane fires are one thing, but this? This is different."

"Different how?" Ivan asked through a cloud of smoke.

"Even the most stubborn arcane fires—you know, those real sticky ones—they go out with enough water. This one hasn't. Sir..." Carver's lips tightened. "I think it's a Fury."

Ivan looked less bored. "A Fury, huh? Why here?"

"I don't know, sir. But if I'm right, we won't be enough to stop it."

The captain stood quietly, gazing into the glowing eyes of the cathedral. "Everyone evacuated?"

"Well, the chapel was empty at the time of the fire, but—"

"Anyone in the city we can call?" Ivan cut him off.

The officer squirmed. "Normally, yes, sir. But there's a problem."

"And that is?"

"He's already inside."

Warren pressed his elbows into the smoldering carpet and lifted his chest from the church floor. Towering flames encircled him, and though they couldn't reach him from where he lay, the heat and smoke were suffocating. His once shining armor was peppered with ash and soot, and the plates along his arms and legs burned against his skin.

The knight craned his neck to stare deeper into the chapel, hoping to find the source of the calamity. There, wreathed in flames, loomed the shallow husk of a skeletal man. A Fury.

The figure was wrapped in leathery, blackened skin, and where its eyes should have been sat two pinpricks of light that burned like the final embers of a dying sun. Its bulky, coal-like armor hung loosely from its frame, rattling and shifting as it held out a vicious, rusty blade toward Warren.

The creature's fleshless jawbone creaked open, and an ancient dusty voice seeped out. "I know you, *heretic*."

Warren dropped his head and huffed. "That right?"

"Oh, yes. *We've* been waiting for you," the figure breathed. "Down below. Waiting to meet the imposter. The liar. The *murderer*."

With a crash, a timber plummeted to the chapel floor, obliterating three pews and bisecting the room with a curtain of cinders. Through the blaze, Warren could see them—those little infernal eyes. They were looking down on him.

"He who wields justice and honor like a rusty dagger," the creature spat. "The one who preaches peace as he harvests souls. How many is it now? Have you kept count? Oh, how your god must be *so proud*."

Warren planted his forehead against the smoking carpet.

"Are you done yet?" Warren groaned.

The knight forced himself first to his knees, then to his feet.

"Look, if I killed you, you must've asked for it. That's on

you. But you made a mistake showing up here. I never leave a job half-finished."

The creature snarled and lunged over the burning timber to stand in the ring of flames encircling the center of the chapel. Warren wiped a layer of sweat and soot from his face and drew his blade.

"You know what the difference is between you and me? When I put you back in whatever hole you crept out of, the people will say, 'We're saved. The monster is dead. All's right in the world.' But when I die?" He paused and spat something red onto the floor. "They'll say that the world's lost a legend."

The armored horror said nothing. The time for talking was over. It held its blade aloft.

Warren stared into the figure's eyes and did not blink. He gnashed his teeth, gripping the hilt of his broadsword with both hands. A sharp wind cut through the sanctuary and whirled against the flames as a wave of radiant light poured from Warren's arms and into his blade. It thrummed with righteous power, burning with starlight and gleaming like diamonds, dwarfing the brilliance of the inferno around them. The Fury took a single step back.

Warren was the knife that cut the tension.

"Let's see which one comes first."

Dawn broke over the city of Bronzebell. As the final traces of smoke wafted from the tattered roof of the cathedral, two figures in red coats made their way inside. The oaken sanctuary doors stood like slabs of charcoal, half off their hinges, groaning in the stillness. Captain Ivan and Officer Carver crept through the space in the door and stood there in the entryway. The captain took it in for a moment, then huffed, shook his head, and lit a cigar.

Had they not known the structure was a chapel before, they wouldn't believe it now. Nothing divine remained. Not a trace of a pew, not a scrap of paper, not even a single swath of a portrait overhead. It was a room with columns and a dais and dozens of piles of wet black ash.

Water dripped from every surface of the place. Steam hissed from the smoldering piles. The windows were gone, and a cool morning breeze found its way through the space and into Ivan's coat.

"They really did a number on this place, didn't they?" Officer Carver asked, picking up a hunk of something that might have been a pew before tossing it back down.

Ivan said nothing and crunched his way deeper inside. The ceilings were mostly barren now. Only a few rough scraps of charred paint clung to the dome here and there. Even the braziers and candleholders sat mangled and warped around the columns as if they'd been crushed within a giant's grip.

Officer Carver gazed up at the ceiling with his mouth open. "So, what do you think happened? Where are they?"

Ivan crossed the room and knelt down. Without looking back, he held up a blackened jawbone for Carver to see.

"Looks like one might've gone back where it came from," said the captain.

Carver plucked the charred bone from the captain's fingers and examined it. "So, he did it then? That's good."

Ivan lifted a long, rusty blade from the floor and flipped it over in his hands.

"Seems that way."

Carver cocked an eyebrow and dropped the jawbone into the ash. "I thought you'd be in a better mood."

"So did I."

Captain Ivan placed the sword back on the wet black carpet and approached the dais. There, standing behind the pulpit, was the charred and battered remains of a statue of the goddess. At its feet was a tablet meant for offerings, but in place of fruit and coins and other miscellaneous things people give up, Ivan found a long, silver sword. Its blade was chipped and cracked, but it was otherwise pristine—seemingly the only item in the chapel free of ash.

"What's that?" Asked Carver.

"A sword," said the captain.

He lifted the blade and made his way back to the pulpit, where a single ray of the morning sun was shining brightly.

Carver was already there, running his fingertips over the surface of the podium.

"And what do you make of this?" He asked.

Ivan had expected to see the ashes of the church's holy text piled there but instead found only a dark soot stain and the indication that it had been brushed clean.

Ivan placed the sword on the podium and took a heavy draw from his cigar.

"Warren's gone," he said through the smoke.

"Gone? Where?" Carver asked.

Ivan shrugged. "Couldn't tell you. But something happened here. Something that made him leave."

The two members of the Arcane Fire Containment Unit stood in the still-hissing, still-dripping room, neither saying much. The door at the other end of the cathedral creaked open, and a swarm of AFCU filed inside. Before long, the room was buzzing.

Ivan took a final puff from his cigar and put it out on the podium.

"That's a shame," Ivan said.

"About Warren, sir?" Carver asked.

The captain nodded. "The guy was a legend."

SHADOW MAGIC

There wasn't much room in Chamomile's little heart for hate. But traps? She *hated* traps. Half limping and half stomping her way down the dim, decrepit hallway, she found a seemingly safe spot between a discolored portrait of a pretentious-looking man and a used-to-be-green buffet table that was coated in a quarter-inch of dust. She planted her back against the wall there and huffed once. The peeling wallpaper rustled like dry leaves as she slid down to examine the tear in her vestments.

Above her left knee, a red stain was spreading in a splotchy circle. The right side of her robe was littered with tiny burn holes, and the smell of charred hair found its way into her nose.

"Here's a fun question," she muttered to herself. She was smiling, but her molars were clenched tightly in the back of her mouth. "How many traps can one person fit into a single three-story house?"

The little halfling twisted her face into a sneer and made her voice deep. "Gee, I don't know Chamomile, how many?"

"*Apparently, a lot!*"

Her shrill voice echoed through the dusty halls as she stamped her foot on the creaky floorboards.

This was supposed to be a simple quest. Just go to the house, grab the book the old wizard wanted, and come back. The necromancer that lived there had been dead for a hundred years. There was nothing to fear. Easy. Simple. Safe.

It had been none of those things. The stupid house where Chamomile found herself having a tantrum had been booby-trapped to high heaven. Every room, every hallway, and even the bathrooms were packed to the gills with all manner of maniacal things that were meant to kill you. She genuinely did not know how you were supposed to shower here without dying.

There were pit traps. There were spike traps. There were traps in the ceiling. Traps in the floorboards. Pressure plates. Falling rocks. Those swingy blade things that come out of the walls with a horrible whooshing sound. There were even nozzles in the floor that shot sizzling columns of fire, which, to her, seemed like a poor choice for a mostly

wooden house that was miles away from any fire depart-
ment. Worst of all, she was pretty sure the entire place was
riddled with black mold. Was that a trap? Not really, but it
certainly couldn't be good for her, either.

Needless to say, the little halfling girl was furious. She
gripped the handle of her mace and thought about
smashing the nearby buffet table. Then she thought of the
dust and guessed that lashing out would just send her into
a coughing fit, which would only make her madder.
Instead, she took a deep breath and tried to unscrunch her
face.

"I swear to the Lightmaker," she said in a mock serene
voice, "If that book isn't in here, Barnabus is going to
pay..."

A pang of guilty fear shot through her chest.

"Double, I mean. He'll pay double. It's not like I
would... you know..." She gripped her holy symbol, made a
whoops face, and got back to her feet.

Up ahead, the corridor turned to the left. She stood in
her safe spot for a moment and held her torch aloft,
searching every possible surface for more traps. She'd
learned by now that cracks and knotholes and little spaces
in the plaster were not so harmless, and she wouldn't be
caught flat-footed again.

Everything seemed clear, so the little cleric carefully
crept to the corner of the hall. With her back to the wall,
she peeked around the edge with one eye, ready to jump
back from a falling axe or a handful of poison darts.

But nothing happened, and there wasn't even that
much to look at. About five feet away, a simple wooden

door with a rusty iron knocker stood beneath a stone arch-
way. In its plainness, it was somehow the most terrifying
thing Chamomile had seen so far. She eased her way out
from behind the wall to stand in front of the door, first
with one foot, then with the other.

She removed the mace from her hip and slid forward,
eyes fixed on the rusty knocker. She knew, beyond any
shadow of a doubt, that the moment she touched the door,
something inexplicably terrible would happen. But what
choice did she have? She'd already searched every room in
the house. This was it. If the book wasn't behind that door,
it wasn't here at all.

With the trembling hands of a first-time cutpurse, she
reached out toward the knocker with her mace. As carefully and slowly as she could, the little halfling lifted the
metal ring with the tip of her weapon, and sure enough,
something did happen. But it wasn't at all what she
expected.

The boards and iron bands of the oaken door rattled,
splintered, and snapped. The fragments of the entryway
shifted and squirmed as a fleshy creature forced its way to
the surface where the planks used to be. It had sores and
bumps all over and a toothy mouth as big as Chamomile's
whole body. Its eyelids peeled back to reveal three weepy,
cat-like eyeballs, and a sticky tongue flopped onto the floor
like a carpet at the halfling's feet. Just as Chamomile raised
her tiny mace over her shoulder to strike at the oozy, door-
shaped monster, its large central eye rolled around to gaze
upon her.

Then, as if its mouth was full of marbles, it spoke in a

labored, gurgling voice. "Those who wish to pass must impress."

With its entire tongue resting on the dusty floor, Chamomile could barely understand it.

She just stood there—stunned—mace still hovering above her.

Neither moved. The fleshy door stared back as a moment of thick silence passed between them. Then its three eyes winced in unison.

"Did you... did you not hear me?" It gargled. "That's okay. I'll try again. Those who wish to pass must—"

The door choked on its own tongue and let out a wet cough. Chamomile's shoulders slumped.

"Sorry, sorry." It cleared its throat. "I was trying to say: Those who wish to pass must impress."

Chamomile placed her mace back onto her hip and pinched the bridge of her nose. "You've got to be kidding me."

"What's the problem?" The door asked.

She didn't answer. She just shut her eyes tighter and took several loud, deliberate breaths.

"Are you... you good?" Asked the door.

Chamomile gave a shallow nod. "Mhmm."

"Okay. It's just that you look super mad right now and—"

"No, no," she cut it off. "No. It's fine. Everything's fine." She exhaled sharply through her nose. "Impress, huh? What does that mean?"

The door's big eye rolled left and right. "Oh, uh... well, I'm not really supposed to give hints or anything. This is supposed to be like, a test or whatever. Listen, if this is a bad time, I can—"

"I *said* it's fine." She shot a vicious look at the door.

Its fleshy form wriggled uncomfortably. "Cool, cool, cool, cool, cool."

If she weren't so furious, so completely and totally done with the day, she might've felt a bit guilty. This thing was an idiot. It probably didn't even know that its master was dead (and had been for a *while* now). She looked the creature up and down, and its eyes blinked at different times in response.

Deciding that this stupid test was better than more traps, she resigned herself to solving the creature's puzzle. She cupped her chin and paced back and forth a bit. What's impressive to a door, anyway?

A few minutes passed. It was hard to think with the raspy breathing of the door in her ears.

"Hey, listen," the door gagged. "Take your time. I've got nowhere to be."

"Could you just—" Chamomile snapped, and the door shrank in on itself. She took another long, deliberate breath, then turned and stomped a bit further down the hall.

Chamomile placed her torch in an empty sconce near the corner of the corridor and continued pacing. Her shadow looked tense. Her shoulders were all scrunched up around her ears. When she relaxed, her neck looked far too long, like a giraffe or a—

The idea hit her like a lightning bolt, and she snapped her fingers.

"Got it!"

The halfling snatched up the torch and crossed the hall toward the door, who shut its eyes and recoiled.

"Here," she said, holding the torch out. "Hold this a second, would ya?"

The door peeled its eyelids open. Then it bulged out from the door frame and took the torch with two of its crusty teeth.

Chamomile sat on the floor and began rifling through her pack. The door looked on in wonder as the halfling took out a small hooded lantern. It was the kind of lamp that was perfect for lighting a small room at the inn, but not so handy when it came to spotting well-hidden traps. She slid a nearby console table into the middle of the hallway and placed the lantern atop it. With a wave of her hand, a small flame appeared inside, and she whipped around to give the door a devious smirk.

"Now then," she hissed.

Chamomile snatched the torch from the door and doused its flame. A brief darkness swallowed the room, and as their eyes adjusted to the dim glow of the flickering lantern, Chamomile took on a wicked expression.

"Have you prepared yourself?" She asked. "I must warn you: Things are going to get strange from here on out. I can't be responsible for what happens next."

The door's three eyes had never been so wide. "Girl, I've gotta tell you, this is super spooky right now. I've got like, a ton of goosebumps, look."

The little cleric passed beneath the table, which was a

few inches taller than her, and twisted her hands together like a fortuneteller.

"Well then," she said, "If you're sure you're ready... Behold!"

As Chamomile's hands shot up in front of the lantern, the shadow of a bunny rabbit appeared on the wall behind her. She wiggled two of her fingers, and its ears bobbed up and down.

"My shadow weaving magic!" She exclaimed.

"Ah, sick!" The door shouted over her. "That's unbelievable!"

"Wait till you get a load of this!"

Chamomile shuffled her hands around to make a spider. Its legs wriggled in the light as she made it walk up the wall. Then she made a bird, then a dog with its tongue wagging, then something that kind of looked like a frog, then another spider. She was running out of animals.

"Huh? Huh?" She asked.

"That's so cool," the door drooled. "Absolutely wild. Hey—you pass. Just go on in."

It shifted its fleshy mass to one side and swung itself open with a slurp.

Chamomile retrieved her lantern and a wide grin spread across her face. "Awesome!"

"Yeah, for sure, for sure. Hey, make sure you look under the old dude's bed. Think there's a vault or something. Seriously, so impressed right now."

The room was dark and dusty, just like all the others. It was full of moldy books and forgotten furniture, and there was a weird smell that seemed to cling to the back of

Chamomile's throat. The door was still talking to itself as she crossed the room toward the bed.

Chamomile knelt down on the floor and peeked underneath. There *was* a vault. It was a small black square embedded into the floorboards, and, chances were, she'd find what she came for inside it. Without thinking, she reached under the bed, wrapped her finger around the handle, and lifted the tiny metal door.

As the latch opened, Chamomile heard a tick. There was a flash in the shadows as a dart flew from the vault and pierced her shoulder. It stung, but the pain was manageable, and she plucked the needle free from her skin.

She rubbed her thumb and index finger together, and a silvery residue spread between them. Poison, if she had to guess. She reached into a pouch on her belt, removed a small vial, and took a healthy swig. It tasted like ginger and pine resin.

Chamomile stuffed the vial back in her belt and made a mental note to take another dose later, just to be safe. She then got back down and shoved her head under the bed to see what she'd found.

Had you asked her fifteen minutes ago how she would've reacted to a poison dart trap right at the end of her quest, she would've given you a very different answer. But for whatever reason, here in the lantern light with the door still happily mumbling to itself across the room, it just didn't seem worth getting angry about.

T here was a light at the end of the tunnel. The shimmering pinhole was weak and gray, far in the distance, and barely visible over the commotion in the corridor, but Ferrin knew it was the way out of this death trap. It had to be.

The grizzled dwarf scrambled for the exit, leaping over stabbing spikes that burst from the floor, dashing through clouds of poison smoke, and ducking beneath rows of arrows flying from tiny slits in the wall. Just a little further now.

"We're nearly there! Don't die on me yet!" He barked over his shoulder.

Ferrin heard a swinging blade shoot out from the wall, and he glanced back to see Lavender slide on her knees beneath it just in time.

"Why? Why are the traps already activated?" She shouted.

The halfling ranger was too short to worry about the arrows firing overhead, but the floor spikes were another story altogether, and she leapt past another set as they shot up toward her stomach.

"Why indeed," said Barnabus. The wizard seemed lost in thought, strolling through the mayhem with a furrowed brow, occasionally extinguishing a flame on the sleeve of his ruby robe.

Rick only roared. His every muscle rippled as he drove his foot straight through a set of wooden spikes, obliterating them and sending splinters flying down the hall toward the others.

"No more traps!"

The light was closer now and growing brighter. Ferrin's lungs were heaving, and his legs were burning, but whatever lay beyond the corridor had to be better than this. He lunged for the opening. Lavender collapsed on the other side along with him. Barnabus trotted out shortly after, and Rick leapt into the room with an altogether unnecessary yell.

Ferrin shot to his knees and glanced around. The hallway of hewn stone had given way to a crystalline chamber, dome-shaped and humming with energy. The walls were thickly crusted in shards of glass-like stone, as thick as tree trunks and pulsing with otherworldly light. The wide, circular floor was mostly barren, except for a small stone dais with a humble altar in its exact center, but it was what floated just above that altar that stole Ferrin's attention.

A shard—a crimson splinter of glass about the length of the dwarf's forearm—spinning slowly in the stillness. Standing just a few feet away, seemingly spellbound by the gem's rotation, was a woman—and Ferrin recognized her. They all did.

"Cosmina?" Barnabus asked.

The corridor of traps behind them sputtered to a halt, and an eerie calm washed over the room. Ferrin could hardly hear the old man's voice. His own heartbeat thumped in his ears, and the crystals around the room emanated a steady hum that vibrated through his chest.

The woman turned to face them, planting an ornate, half-moon staff on the dais. She wore a bejeweled crown of wide-set golden spikes that shot out like sunrays from a featureless mask covering her face. It shimmered like pearls in the pulsing light.

"Barnabus." Her voice flowed like honey, sticky and sweet. "Lovely to see you again, I admit, but I'm really quite busy just now. If you'll excuse me."

The wizard glared at her through a forest of low-hung eyebrows. He wrung his fingers around the knotted body of his staff.

"They deserve to know why, Cosmina. Why send them on this fool's errand?" He asked. "Why have them risk their lives, go through all this trouble, only to betray them now? What could possibly be the point?"

Cosmina placed her palm beneath the hovering shard, tilting her head to one side, then to the other, lost in the glow.

"Do you know what this is, Barnabus?" She asked.

"An artifact," Lavender answered. "An artifact *you* sent us to fetch."

She let out a hollow laugh that made the dwarf's jaw clench. "Too right you are, little one. Is someone frustrated? That was just *dripping* with poison."

"Why don't you skip all this and get on with it?" Ferrin asked. He stood and drew the short sword from his hip.

Cosmina lifted her hand slightly, guiding the shard to

hover before them. It pulsed, and the crimson light danced like a forest fire across her mask.

"Do you know what happens when a god dies? It leaves... traces," she began. "Gods are not so easily forgotten, after all. This is no mere stone, children. This is a sliver of the *divine*."

Ferrin and Lavender shot a glance at one another, then at Rick, who was clearly only half-listening. Ferrin then looked to Barnabus, but the wizard's face revealed nothing. Maybe he already knew the nature of the artifact, but the dwarf had little time to question what it all meant. At that moment, the air changed around them. It was thicker now, cooler.

"You didn't answer the question," said the wizard. "Why now? Why bother sending us here in the first place?"

"It's quite simple, Barnabus. Because you are strong," she admitted. Her tone was that of an adult explaining to a child why they were being punished. "Because had I come here alone, you would have risen to meet me. Maybe not today. Maybe not tomorrow. Perhaps it would've taken years for you to work up the courage, but heroes often find themselves incapable of minding their own business. I want you to see this, *heroes*. I want you to understand—to truly grasp the reality of it all. I want you to know how helpless you are."

With that, Cosmina gripped the shard and slipped it beneath the skin of her arm. To Ferrin's surprise, not a single drop of blood escaped the wound, and a moment later, the crystal vanished entirely.

It happened fast. Too fast. Ferrin started to move, but

before his chest had even leaned over his feet, it was over. The shard was gone.

Barnabus jolted forward. "What have you done? You fool!"

The humming of the crystal dome grew louder, and a fierce wind began swirling throughout the chamber, whipping and whistling against the cavern walls. Cosmina lowered her staff and lifted her chin to peer down her nose at the party.

The exposed skin of her arms and shoulders pulsed. The glow was faint at first, but with each hum it grew brighter, glimmering with something forbidden and arcane. The vortex swirled around her, pulling her long, silver hair toward the ceiling as she rose into the open air.

Then she spoke, and when the voice came, it came not as a whisper, but a clamor—a thousand voices shouting overtop one another, all begging to be heard most clearly. Bellows and shrieks comingled into a single, deafening roar, penetrating Ferrin's ears and mind and chest.

"Mind your tone, *wizard*. That is no way to address a goddess."

Blood boiled in Ferrin's veins, rising up through his neck and burning his ears, but he couldn't recognize the feeling. Was it fear? Anger? He'd been sent here for nothing. His quest had been for nothing. All those months spent researching, exploring, following up on lead after lead after lead—all for nothing. Worst of all, he wasn't even sure who to be mad at.

Was it Cosmina for using them? Barnabus for failing to see through her deception? Then it finally clicked, and

Ferrin felt a wave of pitiful frustration wash over him. His lip curled into a snarl.

It was himself.

He'd done nothing. He just stood there, watching it all unfold like the climax of a play on stage. He didn't even take a step forward or shout "Stop!" He was nothing more than a background character during her monologue, one with a prop sword in his palm, waiting for the star to finish her lines and for the scene to end.

"Now, children," Cosmina said. "*Kneel.*"

This wasn't the deal. This wasn't the quest. This wasn't *fair.*

Ferrin stared at the mechanical left hand dangling by his side. Back when he lost the real one, he spent more than a few nights in some half-forgotten tavern, surrounded by empty flagons and strangers, drinking himself to death—or trying to at the very least.

He wondered why he hadn't stayed there. That could've been the end of it. No more adventures. No more loss. No more nights spent sleeping on the cold dirt or wondering where his next meal would come from. No more begging for shade in the heat of the day or for the warmth of the sun in the dead of night. A simple life—one hand short, sure, but alive. He didn't have to end up here.

There was a man at the other end of the bar during one of those nights. He was surrounded by empty mugs and glasses, missing a hand, same as Ferrin. Turned out they'd both been caught by the same monster, and here they were, sharing more than a drink in a rundown tavern in some godsforsaken village in the middle of nowhere.

He wondered how many nights that man had spent on that barstool, or one just like it. How many times had he ordered the same drinks, free to live well and happy but choosing instead to drown himself in self-pity and ale? Ferrin didn't want that life, either.

So, he made a choice, and he chose this. He chose to follow Barnabus and the others, to get a new arm—to come here. He wondered if he chose wrong. Maybe he wasn't a hero after all.

Something moved in the corner of Ferrin's eyes, snapping him back to the present. It was Lavender—a young halfling woman that stood less than four feet tall. She wore a green cloak and carried a bow fit for a child. But she wasn't kneeling. She was nocking a tiny arrow. Her limbs were shaking, and her lower lip was quivering, but her feet were set.

She was scared. But more than that, she was brave. This little lady with her little bow might have been braver than the lot of them. Ferrin knew one thing for certain, though. She was braver than him.

It was then, in that moment, surrounded by thrumming crystals and buffeted by whipping winds, that the dwarf found something he did not expect to find. Staring down at Lavender's knuckles as they tightened around her bow, just as the fletching reached her cheek—he found courage.

If he was going to live, he was going to live. And if he was going to die, then it would be a death worthy of legend—the kind of death sung by every bard in every tavern in every city across the continent. The kind he might've heard in that bar so long ago. He took a shaky step forward.

"No, I don't think we will kneel," he shouted over the wind. "You've pissed off my little friend here."

Cosmina raked her staff through the air, and a strange, shimmering elixir began bubbling from its end. She pulled the material around her back like a cloak of starlight, and its folds rippled with all the colors of the cosmos. As it flowed, its edges seemed to tug at the fabric of reality, bending the space it passed through, distorting the very air of the chamber.

"Do you think I care?" She asked. "Does a hawk concern itself with the feelings of rabbits?"

Lavender loosed the arrow.

Just as it reached Cosmina's mask, the wooden shaft exploded in the center, and its thousand splinters hung there in the air—motionless, harmless.

"You shouldn't have done that," Cosmina said.

Ferrin shook his head. "Probably not. But you pissed off Rick, too."

Cosmina shot a glance in the barbarian's direction. Barnabus was already standing behind him.

"Go," the wizard said.

With that, he placed his palm against Rick's back, and a swirling arcane seal spread across his skin. In a flash, the roaring barbarian became a crackling streak of lightning that tore across the room toward Cosmina. She raised a barrier of starlight to block the impact, and the lightning ricocheted toward the ceiling.

With a thunderous boom, Rick reappeared directly

overtop the hovering witch, his boots planted firmly against the rocky ceiling. With a fury unlike any Ferrin had ever seen, Rick kicked off the rocks and careened toward Cosmina like a meteor.

His maul sizzled with electricity as he swung down. She raised the barrier once again, but it was no use. The maul shattered the wall of light and crashed into the back of Cosmina's head with a horrific crunch. In a blur, they both plummeted into the stones below, and a plume of dust engulfed the dais.

Silence.

Ferrin watched, breath locked within his chest, waiting for something—a sign, a signal, a shadow of movement. Pebbles rained down upon the stone floor at the dwarf's feet as the dust billowed. Then there was a shift—a strange undulation within the smoke. The space in the center of the room rippled, and a faint glimmer managed to peek its way through the obscurement as a tall, lithe form rose from the floor.

Ferrin took another step, this one stronger. Then he took another and another. His legs seemed to be moving on their own, and before he had time to question them, the dwarf was dashing into the cloud in the center of the room, eyes wide, sword raised.

An arrow whizzed over his right shoulder as he plunged into the smoke, followed by the roar of arcane fire and the boom of Barnabus's voice.

It seemed Cosmina was only half-right. Heroes *were* incapable of minding their own business—but they were anything but helpless.

A VOICE IN THE DEEP

T here was something hypnotic about the descent. As the rusty minecart creaked its way down the forgotten track, Aria found herself lost in the rhythmic ticking of the wheels, the endless vibration of the trolley, and the low rush of stale air as they traveled ever deeper into the earth. The sheer cavern walls were little more than an orange blur to either side. Every now and then, a torch sconce or a lone shovel would appear out of the darkness ahead to race through the lantern light before disappearing once again. Though she'd never considered herself to be claustrophobic, she couldn't help but feel trapped within the bubble of light.

The others didn't seem at all bothered. Ronathon sat on the front of the cart, letting his little legs kick freely over the edge. The halfling carelessly ran a hand through his auburn mohawk, ate a handful of nuts, then picked his teeth clean with the tip of his axe.

Adelphi sat slumped in a frumpy pile in the corner with her robe wrapped around her shoulders. Her cheek was smushed into the side, where a small trail of drool trickled down. Aria amused herself for a moment by counting the crumbs of a half-eaten cookie that still clung to the sorceress's cloak.

Umrick, on the other hand, was keeping busy. Having already sharpened his blade and oiled his armor, the beardless dwarf sat at the back inspecting each arrow in his quiver one at a time. Occasionally, he'd take one out, examine it, shake his head, and sharpen its tip on a whetstone. Then he'd inspect it again, nod, and move on to the next.

So far as she could tell, Aria was the only one growing more uneasy as each minute passed. With every bump and scrape in the track, she braced herself for a creature to lunge out of the darkness toward them or for a shriek to split the perpetual white noise of the rattling wheels, but it never happened. Minutes turned to hours. Hours turned to boredom.

The druidess tried to do the math in her head to figure out how far down they were. They'd been traveling on the same track for nearly three hours now without any change in the walls—no signs, no offshoots, nothing. Only the occasional dusty tool reminded them that someone, anyone, had been down here at one time.

She tried to calculate the angle of the track, the speed at which they were rolling, and the curvature of the spiraling tunnel, but she couldn't focus. With the constant sound and blur, it was almost as if they weren't moving at all.

The further down they traveled, the more the vibration of the cart began to wear on Aria's nerves. It was enough to make even the stoutest adventurer nauseous. She pulled her pack out from beneath Adelphi's leg and removed her apothecary kit. The sorceress hardly stirred as her boot clanged against the metal floor.

"I'm about fed up with this," a gruff voice came from the back of the trolley. Umrick stood for the first time in an hour and stretched his back. "Just how deep are we planning to go?"

"You heard Queen Morel," Aria said. She tossed another pouch of herbs to the side and muttered to herself. "I know I had ginger in here…"

"I did. She said this was the only way into the Autumn Court. She didn't say anything about *this*." He gestured to the darkness.

Aria removed a jar with dusty roots in it. "So, what do you suggest? Hop out and walk back to the surface? Somehow that seems worse. Besides, there's—finally!"

The druidess plucked a thumb's worth of ginger from the kit and cut a slice for each of them.

"To help with the nausea," she explained.

Umrick took it, started chewing, and made a sour face. "Do you think this is it? Is this the... what did she call it?"

"The Forbidden Mines of Unspeakable Horror," Ronathon said in his nasally, monotonous tone.

"Right. How could I forget?" Umrick rolled his eyes.

"And no, I don't think so. I think *that's* it." Ronathon pointed ahead.

Just as Umrick and Aria shifted to see what the halfling was gesturing toward, the minecart lurched forward with a horrible screech and groaned to a stop. Adelphi, for the first time in two hours, shot to her feet.

"Who? Why? What happened?" The sorceress whipped her head left and right, but her eyes were still mostly closed.

A half-second later, she blinked herself awake to find the reason for the others' silence. The trolley had come to a stop in a cylindrical chamber of rough-hewn stone. Straight ahead, looming like a bad omen in the lantern light, was a towering set of black iron doors that rose thirty feet in the air to meet the rugged ceiling.

"This must be the front door," Aria said.

Umrick hopped out of the cart and adjusted his gear. "Guess we better knock then."

The others followed his lead and joined the dwarf in the center of the room. Aria tucked her ancient wooden staff under her arm and reached up to a pocket on her chest. She pinched the fabric and pulled it open slightly to peer down at Nutmeg. The half-asleep chipmunk raised its head and yawned.

"Stay there," she said. "Understood?"

Nutmeg nodded and promptly fell back asleep.

"Good boy. Are we ready?"

"Umrick and I can get the door," Ronathon suggested, trotting toward the right.

"Just be ready for whatever's behind it," Umrick called back. He pressed his hands against the iron, took a breath, then wiped a bead of sweat from his bare cheek. "Unspeakable horror, huh? I thought the name was a joke, but..."

"Second thoughts?" Adelphi asked.

"Just be ready."

With that, Ronathon and Umrick began to push. They grunted with the effort as Adelphi and Aria took up positions near the trolley, staffs at the ready. The titanic doors droned loudly in the chamber, a low rumbling sound that echoed throughout the space and rattled their teeth.

With a grind, the doors cracked and swung open into a deeper darkness than any of the four had ever witnessed. It was as if the light of the lantern didn't dare touch the entrance of the room, and what little glow did was quickly swallowed by an inky blackness that made the hair on the back of Aria's neck stand tall.

Umrick huffed, nocked an arrow, and took a step inside with the others close behind. He looked down at the butterfly brooch on his cloak and whispered, "Scout." Light pulsed from the clockwork insect's wings as it sprang to life. It climbed to the edge of the dwarf's shoulder with a chittering sound and took flight, awkwardly flitting its way into the room. As it sailed deeper inside, a candle flame against the void, Umrick turned toward the others.

"I think we're going to need more light than that."

Aria nodded and hummed an incantation into her palm, where a small fire ignited and hovered just above her glove. Adelphi tapped her staff against the floor twice, and it began to radiate a bright lilac glow. Ronathon cranked the handle of his axe, and the blade burst into oily red flames. In seconds, the area around the party had gone from pitch dark to burning bright, and for the first time, they saw what awaited them in the Forbidden Mines.

It was the floor that caught their attention first—slick, mirror-like black marble cut into six-foot sections. The second was the pillars. Just inside the door stood countless rows of colossal columns—brutal structures carved from the same reflective stone as the floor. They rose beyond the edge of the party's light to meet a ceiling somewhere in the darkness. Aria could just make out the twinkling reflections of their light sources glinting against the tops of the pillars some two-hundred feet overhead. It looked like starlight.

The room was impossibly large, and though their light only penetrated a short distance, the glittering reflections of their flames could be seen far, far in the distance. All around the twinkles was a deep, suffocating darkness—the kind you might expect to find at the bottom of the ocean.

"Which way?" Aria asked.

"This place is enormous," Adelphi responded as if she hadn't heard her. "If you got lost down here, there's no way…"

Aria leaned forward to put herself in the sorceress's line of sight. "Exactly. So which way?"

Umrick cleared his throat. "Let's find out."

The dwarf slung his pack from his shoulder and fished out a jar of oil, affixing it to his belt with the lid removed.

"Aria, do you mind?" He asked, dipping an arrow into the jar.

"Sure thing."

She held out the flame in her palm, and Umrick plunged the arrow inside it. He took a few steps away from the party and scanned the room to the left and right. He found only darkness. With a shrug, he pulled the flaming arrow back and sent it flying to the left.

It sailed through the shadows like a comet, a tail of sparks trailing behind it. The flickering flames highlighted row after row of towering pillars until finally, in the oppressive silence of the room, the arrow clacked against the marble. It might as well have been a cannon shot. The party watched as the arrow burned out hundreds of feet away, like watching a lightning bug wink out for the last time before dawn.

"Not that way, apparently," Umrick frowned.

He repeated the tactic to the right and straight ahead, but each shot revealed only more pillars. Umrick watched as the third arrow, a tiny speck of light in the abyss, fizzled out. He turned back toward the group and shrugged. A moment later, the glowing clockwork insect returned to hover above the dwarf's shoulder.

"Any ideas?" He asked.

Ronathon shrugged back. "How many arrows you got?"

"Enough," Umrick assured him.

"Then let's go. No time to waste," Adelphi said. She took a few brave steps forward, then looked over her shoulder to make sure the others were following.

"Adelphi, mind leaving us a trail?" Aria asked.

"Of what?" She asked.

The druidess waved her fingertips over the ground, and a bundle of flowers slowly swirled into existence.

"Ah," Adelphi nodded.

She affixed her staff to her back and plucked the bouquet from the cold stone floor. Then, without another word, the party began marching into the darkness ahead.

Travel through the mines was slow. Every hundred feet or so, Umrick would hold up a militant hand for the party to stop. He would fire a single flaming arrow to the left, another to the right, and a third ahead of them. When the shots revealed only more pillars, they would continue, silently peering into the shadows every cautious step of the way and collecting Umrick's arrows as they reached them.

After nearly an hour of marching, Aria stopped and let out a loud huff that made Ronathon jump and Adelphi duck.

"What? What is it?" The halfling blurted.

"This doesn't make any sense. I can't be the only one thinking it," she said. Her non-flaming hand shot up to her hip.

"What do you mean?" Umrick asked.

"It seems wrong, doesn't it? Why would a place like this even be here? Think about how long we've been walking. We must be three miles in by now, and nothing? Not a single change? Not a bridge, or a set of stairs, or any indication that we've made any progress at all?"

Adelphi squirmed. "Okay, so what does that mean?"

"What are you thinking?" Umrick asked.

"I don't know, but something seems—"

Run.

Aria froze. It was only a single word, but it burned in the back of her skull like white-hot metal. Something had spoken to her—*inside* her. She *felt* the words as if someone had pressed their lips against her ear and shouted them at the top of their lungs.

Umrick raised an eyebrow. "Aria, you alright?"

The druidess looked down at her hands. They were shaking.

"I... did anyone...?" She muttered.

"Did anyone *what*?" Adelphi asked.

Aria swallowed hard. "That voice? No one else..."

"Oh, nope," Ronathon shook his head violently. "Nope. Nope. That's gonna be a no for me."

Aria scanned the darkness around her. "There was a voice. I'm sure... Was I really the only one that heard it?"

Umrick glanced around. "What exactly did you—"

He stopped suddenly.

"What's wrong now?" Adelphi asked.

He didn't respond. He just stared at a spot on the floor and gripped his bow a little tighter.

"You heard it, didn't you?" Aria asked, crossing toward him.

Umrick nodded slowly.

"Nope. Nope. Nope," Ronathon repeated.

"What did it say?" Adelphi blurted over him.

"It said..." He struggled to get the words out. "Run. It can see you."

"In case I haven't been clear," Ronathon cut in. "No. Absolutely not. I'm out of—"

As the halfling stopped mid-stride, Adelphi let out a small yelp. A quick exchange of glances was all it took to know they'd all heard it.

The party bolted deeper into the room, sprinting past pillar after pillar. Umrick launched flame-kissed arrows to either side as quickly as he could, but they rarely waited long enough to see them land.

"We can't go back," Aria shouted. "There has to be a way out ahead."

Though none of the others would say so, they knew she was right. This was the way to the Autumn Court. Forward was the only option.

It's almost here.

"Don't listen to it!" Umrick shouted as he sent another arrow flying dead ahead.

You must escape. Please.

"Keep moving!" Adelphi cried, tossing handfuls of flower petals behind her. "There must be another exit."

It's watching. It won't stop. Run.

"What part of 'unspeakable horror' did you guys not hear?" Ronathon screamed. He was sprinting with his eyes closed.

It's coming. It won't let you out.

By now, they were all gasping for air. Aria's side burned like a dagger had been thrust between her ribs. Finally, she slid to a halt and threw her hands onto her knees.

"Stop! Just... stop!" She huffed.

The others stumbled into one another and spun around to face her.

"Are you okay?" Umrick called back.

"Am I *okay*?" She spat. "No. No, I'm not okay. What are we doing?"

The other three exchanged glances.

"Running for our lives?" Ronathon asked.

"From *what*?" Aria tossed her hands up in the air. "Have we seen anything? Anything at all?"

Umrick stared into the darkness behind her.

"Have we heard anything? Smelled anything?"

No one answered.

"I think it's screwing with us. I think it's a trick—and I

think we're falling for it," she said, finally calm enough to look each of her companions in the eye.

The four stood in the silence, bathed in the glow of their collective light. Though the darkness still beat down against them, it felt lighter somehow. Umrick let out a chuckle, the kind you might hear when two strangers try to pass one another but keep dipping in the same direction.

"Maybe you're right," said the dwarf. "What are you thinking, illusion magic? Maybe it's nothing but pillars after all."

The flames from the arrow nocked in Umrick's bow began to lick at his glove, so he sent it flying lazily toward the left to be rid of it. He didn't even pull the bowstring back all the way. The four watched the arrow sail through the darkness, passing more identical columns and casting a dull glow along the floor. There was some kind of catharsis in its flight, as if the arrow itself proved their point. As if it landing out there in the nothingness was all the evidence they needed that the room was empty—that it always had been.

Whatever the voice was, wherever it had come from, it was a trick. It was meant to deceive them—to convince them that randomly sprinting into the darkness was the only way to escape, but it hadn't worked. They had a trail leading back to the door. They had light. They had everything they needed. They were nearly fooled, but this arrow was proof that they wouldn't fall prey to cheap tricks again.

The fiery arrow reached the end of its flight and clinked

against the ground. As it slid to a halt, the dying flame washed over something—something standing in the center of the floor between two columns.

It was a man, nude and misshapen. Its arms and legs were long and spindly, bent back against themselves in a sickening posture. Its jaw hung too low, stretching down toward its navel where a row of thick white teeth sat crooked above its breastbone. Its eyes were nothing more than black pits above a set of sunken cheeks. Wisps of hair shot out like weeds from its wrinkled scalp.

Just as the flickering light winked out, the creature bent backward and darted toward a nearby column on all fours. In the newfound darkness, each of them heard the unmistakable slap of skin against stone as it clambered away.

I warned you.

Aria's legs turned to stone. The words scraped at the back of her mind like rusty claws, and she couldn't manage to take a full draw of air. She peeled her eyes away from the wall of darkness, praying the others were still in high spirits—that it was another trick and that she had been the only one to see that *thing* out there in the abyss beyond the light.

But they had seen it, and she knew it without needing

to ask. It was there, written on their ghostly expressions, plain as day. Umrick and Adelphi were frozen like Aria, but Ronathon was shaking his head back and forth with his eyes shut.

He shoved past the others.

"Enough! I'm sick of caves. I'm sick of the dark. I'm sick of voices in my head, and I'm sick of whatever the hell that thing was. I'm going out there. I'm gonna find it, and I'm gonna kill it. You can either stay here or help me. I don't care which."

Something about the little halfling's blunt rage sparked a sense of calm cynicism inside Aria. It was a comfortable feeling. The fear that had been draped over her body like a wet sheet was suddenly yanked away.

What was she so afraid of exactly? This was certainly no worse than anything else they'd faced so far—it was just darker. It didn't matter how unsettling the creature was; it was *one* creature. They could handle one creature. Imagine if she'd frozen up like this against that last dragon. This was no time to fall apart, and the others felt it too.

Ronathon seemed to sense the shift in his companions. Wordlessly, he turned and sprinted into the darkness, beyond the edge of the others' light, and was instantly swallowed by the shadows. The glow of his axe disappeared around a pillar. The other three nodded once at each other, took a collective breath, and started marching.

"It's over here!" Ronathon shouted from somewhere beyond the light.

Aria gripped her staff and started to call out to him, but just as the words reached her lips, the voice shot into her mind once more. It was a simple message; one delivered a single word at a time with perfect and horrible clarity.

That's. Not. Ronathon.

T his wasn't the first time Ceveral had awoken face down on a cold stone floor (and should he have it his way, it wouldn't be the last). He let out a half chuckle, and the small puddle of grimy water against his lips rippled in the darkness.

"Must've been quite a night," he sighed, lifting himself to his knees.

His head was pounding. As he raised his torso from the floor, he expected to see the legs of a bed frame, a chest full of blankets, maybe even an armchair. He imagined seeing the room filled with empty wine bottles and half-eaten appetizers on a dirty platter. He thought he might even find a few errant partygoers still snoozing softly around the room.

He found none of those things. Just stone walls that wept water from every conceivable pore, pockets of slimy lichen beneath his palms, and a deep, pervasive darkness.

In that fraction of a moment, as his pupils grew wide in search of light, he realized something that brought a heavy lump toward the top of his throat.

Ceveral had no idea where he was.

The room was small, with low, wet ceilings that gave the impression it was raining inside. He could hear the droplets pattering against the stone around him, and he became all too aware of his soaked-through clothes.

To his left, he could just make out the shape of a door, but the outline of thick and rusty iron bars brought him no comfort. His heartbeat crashed against his breastbone, and, almost on instinct, he fumbled for the dagger on his belt. His fingers found only wringing-wet cotton.

"No such luck, I'm afraid," a voice called out from the darkness behind him.

Ceveral fell to his backside and scrambled toward the wall.

"Stay back—what is this? Where am I?" He blurted.

An inky shape floated closer and hovered above him.

"Who are you? What do you want?"

The figure loomed there for a moment, a shadow within a shadow, then slowly lowered itself to meet him.

"A friend," it said gently. "And I want you to lower your voice."

Like a springtime sunrise, a warm and gentle glow spread throughout the room. There, kneeling before him, was a well-dressed man with reddish skin and burgundy eyes. A tiny ball of saffron light hovered just above the tip of his index finger. He had a pair of curled charcoal horns that extended from his forehead, and his dark hair was pulled back in a damp, stringy ponytail.

Ceveral studied his face carefully—the creases at the corners of his eyes, his sharp brows, the warmth of his skin —but he was certain of it. He'd never seen this man before in his life.

"You've been unconscious for two days," the stranger said quietly. "I thought you might be dead." He stared at the wall above Ceveral's shoulder. "Then again, maybe that would have been for the best."

Words flew from Ceveral's mouth before he could catch them. "I don't understand. Who are you? What is this? Where are we?"

The stranger blinked a few times.

"I've never known you to be this dramatic," he paused. "What am I saying? Of course, I have." Something like a laugh came out.

"What are you talking about?" Ceveral asked, doing little to disguise the wave of frustration that passed through him. "I don't even know who you are."

"Your memory is gone, isn't it, Ceveral?" The man asked. "It'll return shortly. At least, it did for the rest of us."

He gestured toward a group of people huddling in the corner of the small stone room, at least a dozen of them, of all shapes and sizes and ages.

They were filthy. A dwarf with half his beard missing stood shirtless and shivering. An elf with a black eye sat away from the others, his tunic torn and dripping in the lowlight. A halfling girl peered around the legs of an elderly human.

Ceveral couldn't decide if they were trembling from the cold or fear, but, either way, he didn't think he could blame them. He was shaking too.

"I know this will mean very little at the moment, but I need you to listen to me." The stranger snapped his fingers in front of Ceveral's face until their eyes met. "My name is Poet, and you and I are close friends."

Ceveral shook his head. "I don't understand, I—"

"Please," Poet held up a hand. "There's no time. We were traveling with another, a gnomish girl. Her name was... *is* Marigold. Sound familiar?"

Ceveral shook his head again.

"That's unfortunate," Poet said. "We were taken—the three of us. I don't know where to. But that doesn't matter." He said the next part in a hush. "Because I can get us out of here. We just need to find Marigold first. Do you understand?"

Ceveral sat still for a moment, then slowly nodded. "Taken..." He hesitated. "Taken by who?"

A furious, gurgling screech, like a goose being slaughtered by a dull knife, echoed down the hall. Then the frantic slapping sound of fleshy feet against stone came rushing into the cell.

The light in Poet's hand winked out. Darkness swallowed the prison.

"By them," he whispered.

Something wet slammed against the bars—hard. As the creature lifted a glowing hunk of coral to its face, the acid in Ceveral's stomach rose with it. The warbling, slimy thing beyond the door had the arms and legs of a man, but atop its shoulders was a gasping, gulping fish head.

It whipped its face back and forth, peering into the cell with one glassy eye, then the other. As it fumbled for a set of rusty keys on its hip, its bulbous lips curled back to reveal a row of jagged yellowing teeth. It barked back down the hallway.

The shrieking grew louder. The key turned. The door opened. And then, they were upon them.

. . .

Ceveral and the other prisoners had wet bags pulled over their heads before being led through a labyrinth of passageways. At least half a dozen fish-headed creatures marched alongside them, gasping and screeching, prodding them with spears and tridents as they blindly marched.

Ceveral's head was still spinning, so he latched onto the one familiar thing he could find: Poet's voice. Though the half-stranger's chest was nearly pressed against Ceveral's back as they walked, his voice trickled through the wet burlap like a distant conversation in a crowded bar. He could only just make out the words.

"Stay calm," Poet whispered. "We will get out of here. I promise. Just find Marigold. Stay focused. Try to remember. Can you do that for me?"

When they finally came to a halt, the fish-headed creatures shoved the prisoners against one another in a cluster. Ceveral could feel other bodies, trembling and warm, pressed against him on all sides.

When the bag was violently pulled from his head, Ceveral found their small group was no longer alone. They stood packed like cattle with at least fifty other prisoners in the center of a colossal, well-lit cavern.

Glowing coral of all shapes and sizes climbed up the nearly six-story walls, and a colony of stalactites wept rain from overhead. The cavern was the size of a small city, and huge columns of stone rose from the floor to support the ceiling. Lining the walls and columns were stairs and doorways, windows and balconies. It *was* a city. Ceveral's eyes followed one of the pillars toward the cavern roof, and as his head tilted back, he felt his stomach plummet into his boots.

There, in the center of the ceiling, was an opening—a massive hole the size of a town square. Suspended in that hole, high above the cavern floor, was water. They were looking at the bottom of the ocean, but, for whatever reason, the water did not fall. It simply rippled gently overhead.

Ceveral could see light—sunlight—fighting its way from the surface of the sea high above. He could almost feel it glistening against his skin. Almost.

To his left, Poet stood similarly transfixed—though his gaze was locked on something much lower to the ground. Ceveral followed it.

Just ahead of them was a round opal dais bearing a bleach-white throne. Standing before the throne, hovering above the crowd, was a priestly creature with steepled fingers. The human-like thing was clad in tight-fitting black robes that revealed its skeletal frame, and its skin was like rice paper—purple veins throbbing just beneath the surface. In place of a head, however, there was a spiny, black sea urchin the size of a beer barrel that rested precariously atop a long, spindly neck.

It spread out its arms and began speaking, Ceveral assumed. Its voice resonated in a shrill, whale-like call that made the prisoners' eyes water. The priest gestured to the group where Ceveral stood, then motioned across the room to a second mass of prisoners. Ceveral hadn't even noticed them until now.

As the urchin priest's droning voice reached a climax, it turned and peered at the ceiling, spreading its arms out once more with a flourish—as if begging to be embraced by something.

In the shimmering waters suspended overhead, a dark, inky cloud swirled, slowly enveloping the entire window into the sea. The now blackened ocean began to bulge inward, forming a murky bubble that reached down toward the slack-jawed prisoners—but it did not burst. It hung in the cavern air like a colossal teardrop, swelling and rippling above the cavern floor. The shadowy outlines of fish could be seen scrambling in the blackened waters.

Then another shape appeared. Titanic. Writhing.

A tree-sized tentacle burst from the bubble and flailed wildly in the open air of the undersea chamber. It moved with the violent alacrity of a bullwhip. Then another appeared. Then another.

Ceveral watched—paralyzed—as eight immense tentacles escaped the water and thrashed in every direction. The prisoners ducked low to the ground to avoid their sweeps, but one man—a young human—was too slow. A tendril collided against him and wrapped around his legs, plucking him from the crowd and reeling him into the swelling abyss overhead.

As he screamed and clawed for the safety of the floor, a dark mass bulleted its way through the ink and burst forth with a dissonant roar that shook the coral clinging to the cavern walls. The crustaceous beast flung the unlucky man into its maw—swallowing him whole without so much as a crunch.

The urchin-headed priest chirped with glee, steepling his fingers once again. The half-obscured leviathan above them scanned the crowds with unfeeling eyes, drooling something viscous onto the stones below. It stopped as it reached Ceveral's group.

The priest released a final, humble whirring sound—the "amen" at the end of his sermon.

There was a pause. A single moment of stunned silence.

Things moved quickly after that.

In a flurry of screams and roars, tentacles slammed into the prisoners around Ceveral, crushing the stone beneath them and sending rocky shrapnel in every direction. A shard found its way into Ceveral's side, but he hardly noticed the pain. Too much was happening.

The crowd around him thinned as people were ripped from the ground one after another, some devoured, others sent careening into the walls like stones from a catapult. One minute they were a person. The next, they were a small red stain on the wall in the distance.

A hand gripped Ceveral's frozen shoulder.

"We have to find Marigold! Move!" Poet screamed.

But it was too late. A leathery tendril wrapped around Poet's chest and stole him into the sky. Ceveral watched it in slow motion. Just as Poet was thrust into the beast's jaws, he mouthed something. Two clear words.

His burgundy eyes were wild—burdened with grief.

I'm sorry.

Then, he disappeared from the creature's grip. Not eaten—just gone. Vanished. He was there one moment and not the next, and suddenly Ceveral found himself standing alone beneath the writhing shadow of the kraken.

Ceveral had two choices then. The first and most obvious was to die. The second was to run—and almost certainly still die. He chose the latter.

He tore off to the left side of the cavern. A tentacle smashed into the floor in front of him, snatching up another unlucky prisoner. Ceveral didn't stop. He kept running, faster and faster. Another tendril swung low and raced toward him. He dove to the ground and covered his head, smashing his chin on the rocks. The tentacle passed overtop him, and in a blink, he was back on his feet and sprinting again.

Others were running, too. He tripped over an elf as they knelt down to tug at an elderly man on the ground. Ceveral glanced back at the pair of them. He wished he hadn't. They were gone before he reached his feet.

He barreled toward the cavern wall where dozens of openings led into darkness, but in the chaos, he didn't stop to consider where they would take him. It was somewhere other than here, and that was enough.

Ceveral darted into a pitch-dark tunnel, and the horrific sounds behind him changed. The sharpness of the screeches and screams dulled to a deeper, sadder hum. He took a left, then a right. He descended a set of grimy stairs, then took another left.

Before long, his pace slowed. His legs were sluggish and heavy now, and his chest was on fire. It was like his lungs couldn't find enough air. He was more than lost now. Wherever he was, it was dark. The only light to be found came from the occasional chunk of glowing coral haphazardly wedged into the wall. He found one, pressed his back against the stone beneath it, and took several long, shaky gasps. His clothes were soaked, and his hair was sticky, but he didn't know if it was sweat or something worse. He didn't intend to find out.

What was he supposed to do now? He'd escaped the kraken, sure, but now what? Poet was gone. His one way out was gone too. He didn't even know what that gnomish girl looked like or what help she could be at this point anyway.

Something scratched at the back of Ceveral's mind—a feeling that didn't quite feel like his own. It told him to find Marigold. After another minute in the dark, he conceded. It's not like he had any idea how he was meant to get himself from the bottom of the ocean to the top again. Maybe she did.

Just as Ceveral began to wonder how he was supposed to find a single person in this pitch-black labyrinth, a nearby shriek rippled down the hallway. One of them was coming. Maybe more than one. The slapping sound of their webbed feet grew louder.

Ceveral ducked out of the light and searched the wall for something—anything—to help him. He found a door handle. It was a simple, rusty knocker. He slammed his shoulder into the door and fell inside, then kicked it shut again, wincing as the slam echoed against the walls.

Slap. Slap. Slap.

Ceval shut his eyes tight.

Slap. Slap. Slap.

The sound was closer now, moving toward the door.

Slap. Slap. Slap.

Ceval let out something like a silent prayer, hoping that whoever was listening would cut him a break.

"Please. Please just let it pass. Let it keep walking. Please."

Slap.

The creature stopped in front of the door. Ceval could hear it gulping air just on the other side.

The seconds ticked by like weeks.

Ceval held his breath.

Then the door burst open. The fish-headed thing scrambled in and threw itself on top of Ceval. His head slammed against the wet stone as the monster's full weight collided against him. Its slimy hands pressed into his shoulders and face as it fumbled for its weapon, wailing like a banshee in the dark. Ceval kicked and screamed, and the thing screeched louder.

Then there was a different sound—one Ceval didn't recognize. Something like a sharp slurp.

The fish-thing stopped fighting. Its arms and legs went stiff. Then they went limp. With a final wet gasp, it fell to the floor beside him with a thud.

Ceval scurried back in the darkness.

In the doorway, there was a spark, and that spark crackled into a small flame. It was a torch, and holding that torch was a girl, not much bigger than a human child. She pulled back a hood that was far too large for her and peered across the room at him.

"Ceveral?" She asked. "It's me—Marigold."

He managed to choke out a single word. "Marigold?"

"Yep. Memory still gone?"

He nodded.

"Great. Can you stand?"

It took more effort than it should have, but Ceveral managed to get to his feet. He stared down at the fish-headed thing.

"It's dead," Marigold said. "We need to move. I know how to get out of here."

Ceveral's heart felt like it'd been ripped in half and sewn back together in an instant. Grief and fear and relief swelled inside his chest, and he couldn't tell which was which anymore. It was the first thing other than pure confusion and outright terror that he could remember feeling since he awoke in the cell. It wasn't an altogether good feeling, but it was something, and, for a reason he couldn't explain, he trusted this little girl. He knew she could get him home safe.

"Grab anything useful you can find," Marigold said, "And don't relax yet. Our work isn't done. First thing's first, we have to find someone."

Ceveral had just started to pry open a half-rotted crate but stopped. His body went numb. "Find someone? Who?"

Marigold was searching the creature's body. A confident smirk flashed across her face in the torchlight.

"A friend of ours. A man named Poet. He's our way out."

ARTEMIS PARK

There is little hospitality to be found in The Farther. The sunbaked wasteland of shattered red clay extends for hundreds of miles, a sprawling nothingness of dusty riverbeds without shade, without water, without relief.

From its fiery center, the crimson fields stretch toward the horizon like the blistered, sunburnt skin of a withering god, and illusions plague the eyes of travelers who stare too longingly in any one direction. At night, when the sun abandons The Farther, there is no comfort to be found in its absence. The barren stretch becomes a mirror world of deep purples and biting winds, and the once searing heat plummets into a deathly chill.

The living things that manage to carve out some meager existence within this furnace are few and far between, mostly bone-dry shrubs with stinging thorns and poison seeds. The only other inhabitants to be found are the monolithic buttes of blood-red stone that rise sharply toward the cloudless sky, looming over the shattered ceramic beneath them.

No one goes to The Farther by choice. No one but Lavender, that is.

The little halfling stood on the splintered wooden deck of an unnamed airship, bundled tightly in a puffy coat and several scarves. The night sky glistened like rubies and sapphires overhead, and a pale moon poured its gaze down upon the arid earth several hundred feet below the ship.

With her back against the railing, the whipping cold buffeted the young ranger, and she tugged at the wool around her neck to cover her chapping cheeks. The tiny bow upon her back had just begun to crust with frost when a gruff voice hollered from the wheel.

"Ain't much farther now. No pun intended, I guess."

The captain of the dilapidated ship was a short man with leathery skin, wiry iron whiskers, and very few teeth. He didn't speak much and offered no indication as to where exactly he was taking her, but his eyes remained trained on the horizon, rarely looking away from a seemingly specific spot that Lavender couldn't make out.

She shoved a shivering hand into one of her deep pockets and removed a folded piece of parchment. The edges were soft and beginning to fray after opening and refolding the note a few too many times. She'd memorized the message long ago, and though she knew it would do no good, she took to unfolding it once again. Maybe she missed something.

Lavender,

Barnabus spoke highly of you. We could use someone with your talents. Come to Artemis. There will be a ship waiting for you tomorrow night. The sooner, the better.

Best,
—M

Lavender's eyes scanned the letters for the hundredth time, yet, once again, she was left with the same basic questions. What is Artemis? Who is M? And, of course, the one that she was no stranger to asking:

"What exactly have you gotten me into this time, old man?" She whispered to herself.

There was a familiar feeling twisting up her insides. Not fear, precisely, but something akin to apprehension. Though she'd come to consider Barnabus a great friend, the wizard seemed to have a way of dragging her into situations that skirted the line between dangerous and outright deadly. If their most recent travels together were any indication, this little adventure promised to be more of the same.

Lavender turned to peer over the railing and sighed. The captain yanked on a rusty lever, and two bright columns of fire burst into the lumbering red balloons that drifted above the deck. For a moment, the heat of the flames spread across her back, but the frigid wind quickly found its way back beneath her coat.

"There it be," said the captain, pointing dead ahead.

The sun was just beginning to creep its way toward the horizon, and the deep dark of the night had lifted to a murky lilac that drenched the land below as far as the eye could see. Lavender shivered her way to the bow but saw nothing. There were no towns, no structures, no traces of anything even resembling civilization. Just endless shattered clay and stoic plateaus that eyed her suspiciously as she floated past.

She looked back at the captain as if to ask, "Where, exactly?" He pointed forward once again to the east.

Lavender peered at the spot but saw only a single dark cloud looming in the distance, a small, thin shadow against an otherwise featureless sky. As the ship bobbed its way onward, the shape grew clearer, larger. It wasn't a cloud at all but rather a titanic plateau that stretched across the dead center of the desert. It dwarfed the surrounding buttes and spires, with sheer walls that rose higher than the ship itself, and overhead, the rocky cliffs disappeared into a ring of billowy fog that covered the entire top like a powdered wig.

She folded the note and shoved it back into a pocket,

retrieved her bag, and prepared to land. To her surprise, the ship did not descend, nor did it rise any higher. It continued its lumbering journey straight ahead.

Just when Lavender thought the ship might collide with the cliff face, she spotted a dull, metallic shimmer in the shade. It was a platform, a wide square of steel that jutted out from the side of the rock. There were two small docks on the right side, a tiny featureless building, and a metal railing that seemed to be doing its best to offer some semblance of safety.

A few minutes later, the ship creaked to a stop and locked into place several hundred feet above the desert floor. Lavender thanked the captain, whose name she had not thought to ask, and carefully stepped down onto the platform. The next moment, the ship spewed fire, hoisted itself aloft, and was gone.

A dreadful wind whipped against the structure, which groaned in response, shifting a bit beneath the halfling's feet. Lavender scanned the area for someone to greet her but found no one, not even a trace of a someone.

"Hello?" She called.

The wind whistled a reply. The door to the small structure at the back of the platform was locked, so she made her way toward the other side. Here, there was a split in the cliff face, a deep square crevasse with a long metal railing embedded into its center. It rose sharply toward the sky before disappearing into the fog. Lavender followed its path down to an area of the floor outlined in yellow paint and surrounded by a low metal railing. There were words written there, repeating a short phrase:

WARNING: PLEASE ALLOW THE PLATFORM TO COME TO A

COMPLETE STOP.

It was then that she noticed a small control panel at the back of the platform. It was covered in buttons and small, blinking lights, all labeled with words she didn't quite understand. With no one around to tell her otherwise, she picked the large green one on the left and pressed it with her palm.

The platform within the platform whirred to life and began to rise. The ascent was slow but not altogether safe feeling. Lavender found herself clinging to the railing at the back for most of the ride. As the platform pressed into the dense fog above, she was glazed in dew, and the bite of the cold sunk a bit deeper into her bones.

It wasn't long before the lift came to a grinding halt. Two gates popped open on the railing at the back, and Lavender exited into a circular courtyard surrounded on all sides by tall, crimson cliffs. The floor of the place was carved from white stone, neat and tidy, and ahead stood a long staircase of similar craftsmanship that cut deeper into the rock. The top of the stairs melded into the fog, obscuring what awaited beyond.

The little halfling removed the bow from her back but did not yet draw an arrow. Though she was now acutely aware of her situation—alone, no way down, and nowhere to go but up—she did not want her first impression to be that of an ungrateful or skeptical guest, should this turn out to be something *other* than a trap.

She then trotted across the courtyard and up the stairs,

which climbed at least a hundred feet before opening to a long and wide hallway with shorter walls. Through the mist, she could just make out the now grayish sky above. The walls were lined with simple stone benches, a few potted plants, and a couple of trash cans. Ahead stood a tall wrought-iron gateway with two wide doors and an arched sign which read:

WELCOME TO ARTEMIS PARK

Lavender stared at the words for a long time, and her head spun.

"A... park?" She asked herself. "Here? Who in their right mind would—"

Her questions were cut short by the creaking, metallic sound of the gate. The right door swung open just enough, and someone stepped out into the entryway.

It was a woman in heavy silver armor. The layered steel plates clanged and rattled as she slid free from the door. She wore a white cape that brushed against the tile beneath her, and atop her head was a mess of frizzy chestnut hair that stopped just above her shoulders. The woman stood there, quickly dusting off her armor (which did not appear to be the least bit polished), then took to smoothing her hair into place. It was then that she looked up for the first time, saw Lavender, and froze at once.

"Oh. You're... already here," she said. Her voice was kind and soft, if not more than a bit flustered. She seemed unsure of what to do with her hands. "Right. Well. Follow me, then."

With that, she turned on her heels, disappeared behind the gate, and clanked away. Lavender scratched her head, then scurried after her, opting to keep her bow in her hand for now.

She wasn't sure what she expected to find on the other side, but the sight was befuddling, nonetheless. It *was* a park—an extraordinarily clean and well-kept one at that. The entryway was tiled with the same white stone, and the gate was flanked with four cozy-looking buildings.

There was a welcome center with a ticket counter, a tea shop that sold frozen yogurt, a small café with several outdoor seats, and even a gift shop. Up ahead, the armored woman was walking with purpose. She'd already made her way through the elegant courtyard ahead, the corners of which were dotted with young oak trees. Lavender didn't know where to look first, so she hurried on, calling after the lady.

"Hey, wait! Hey!"

She tried to run past the trickling fountain in the center of the square but hesitated when she noticed the masterfully carved statue that sat atop it. The stonework featured animals and creatures, dozens of them—a dragon soaring, a lion roaring, a horse galloping, several fish leaping through the air, and many more that Lavender didn't have time to take in. Each of the carvings shot a tiny arc of water from its mouth, trickling into the basin below with a pleasant dribble.

By now, the woman was crossing another open area that held dozens of tables and chairs beneath the shade of pink and blue umbrellas. On either side, the park opened up to snake its way along railed pathways that disappeared around the corners.

There were bronze signs, too, but in the still-thick fog, Lavender couldn't make them out from where she stood. As she raced to catch up with the armored stranger, she passed by a particularly fancy sign that stopped her in her tracks. In big black letters it read:

DIRECTORY
Dragons & Dragonkin →
Oozes & Slimes ←
Elemental Exhibit →
Aviary ↑

She called ahead again, still staring at the board.

"Hey! Wait! What is this?"

When she finally peeled her eyes away from it, the woman had nearly disappeared into the fog. Lavender sprinted after her once again, taking several confused glances back at the sign. The woman finally stopped in the center of a raised platform beyond the courtyards and turned to wait. By the time Lavender reached the top of the stairs, she was quite out of breath and placed her hands on her knees.

"Hold on... Just... What is all this? Who are you? Where are we?"

The woman stared with a blank expression. She had dark bags under her eyes, and her frizzy hair had popped back into a mess in the wind. She blinked several times.

"I'm… I'm sorry, did you… did you not receive my letter? You must have. You're here, after all."

Lavender rifled through her pockets and handed it over. "You mean this?"

The woman unfolded it and scanned the words. She mumbled them to herself, then stopped short and pinched the bridge of her nose.

"Oh," she groaned. She dragged her fingertips down her face, stretching the skin under her eyes. "Okay. Okay. Wow. I'm afraid I owe you an apology, Lavender. This didn't tell you much of anything, did it?"

The halfling shook her head.

"Forgive me. I… haven't been sleeping much. It seems that deprivation has found its way into my penmanship, hasn't it?"

Lavender fluttered her eyes, still thoroughly lost. "No, it's fine. I'm just trying to understand what this is."

The woman cleared her throat and stood tall. "Allow me to start over with a proper introduction: My name is Millicent, and I'm the director here."

"Okay, but where is *here*?"

At this, a blustering wind rushed across the top of the butte, stirring the fog around them into a flurry. The sun had only just broken free from the horizon, and as the piercing light cut across the sky, it seemed to carry the mist itself along with it.

"See for yourself," Millicent said.

Beyond the edge of the dais, which stood high above the plateau below, was a spellbinding landscape that stretched for at least a hundred miles. Every square inch of the plateau's top was covered in a kaleidoscope of habitats, dozens of them, all butted up against one another and overlapping at the seams. Plains, savannahs, and meadows crawled toward a snow-peaked mountain range to the west. The fresh powder of a recent avalanche glittered in the morning sunlight.

In the center were deep jungles and lush forests, with darker patches of mires and swamps that dotted the verdant greenery. There was water, too—lakes and ponds that snuggled up to the edges of vast woodlands, and rivers and streams crisscrossed in a labyrinth over it all.

To the east, rugged cliffs and crevasses—arid wastes and towering spires. In the far distance gleamed the platinum tops of sandy desert dunes. Beyond it all, crisp blue sky and a few fluffy clouds that rolled and churned just above the plateau top, but nowhere else.

There was life here, more than Lavender could ever recall seeing. Packs and herds of familiar beasts slowly crept their ways across the habitats, and flocks of common birds swooped down toward the many shores scattered about the place.

There were stranger sights as well: Enormous hunting birds that spiraled above the plains in wide arcs; leathery creatures with scales that walked on two legs and four, some of which had necks as long as a fishing boat; and titanic bugs buzzed above the jungle canopies before swooping into the leaves.

"Welcome to Artemis Park," said Millicent. "Conservation Center for the Fey and Foreign."

Lavender's head spun. How did this place get here?

Why was it here? Why was *she* here? The sprawling habitats that stretched out before her couldn't be natural, could
they? That would mean someone put them here. But who
could be powerful enough to...?

"Beautiful, isn't it?" Millicent asked.

The little ranger said nothing, but she managed to
close her mouth and give a quick nod in agreement.

"Ah, before I forget," the director began, jamming a
gauntleted hand into her pocket. "Barnabus asked me to
give you this once you arrived."

Millicent held out an envelope, and Lavender tore into
it, unfolding the letter in the still-whipping wind.

Little one,

*First, allow me to apologize for all the trouble I've
caused you over the years. It's been a bit of a mess,
hasn't it? I still feel awful about that business with the
giant.*

*Then again, it wasn't all bad, now was it? I rather
enjoyed our little chats on that voyage, and I seem to
recall you have a particular fondness for the creatures of
this world. I may have passed on a story or two to Millicent here. I hope you don't mind.*

*Please consider this as much an apology as it is a heart-
felt thank you. The world is safer because of you,
whether you know it or not. I'll do my best to let you*

work in peace, my friend. Though, if I'm honest, adventure does seem to have a habit of finding us, now doesn't it?

See you soon,
—Barnabus the Resplendent

A chill nipped at Lavender's cheek, and she raised a hand to soothe the sting. It was a tear.

"Alright, dear?" Millicent asked.

Lavender rubbed her face with the back of her glove and sniffed sharply. "Yeah. To be honest, I'm not even sure why I'm crying."

The director gave a knowing nod. "That tends to happen at times like this."

"Times like this?" Lavender asked.

"When one adventure ends, and another begins."

Lavender stood in the stillness of the morning, gazing out over the great plateau top, feeling the sunrise against her skin and the wind upon her cheeks. She read the note once more, then folded it up and placed it in her pocket. A moment of silence passed between them before the director's words finally settled into the front of the halfling's mind.

"Wait, another adventure?" She asked. "What do you mean?"

"Isn't it obvious?" Millicent asked.

As Lavender looked up, the wind lifted the director's

hair away from her shoulders. It was redder than she had thought, whipping like ruby fire in the shining dawn. For the first time, Lavender noticed a platinum gleam at the edges of the woman's armor. Millicent turned and extended a hand down toward her.

"I'd like to offer you a job."

A labaster had gorged itself on academia. The city sat fat and bloated with universities and colleges, all packed into nooks and crannies and stacked on top of each other, sometimes three buildings high. You couldn't throw a stone without hitting a marble column.

Some were as large as a village, others were as cozy as a tea shop, and Dr. Fenwick Frazzlefoot had been hired, fired, and rehired by each of them at least once.

You might not think Fenwick so remarkable if you saw him sprinting from one campus to the next with his leather briefcase clutched to his chest and a swarm of loose papers trailing behind him like a cloud of lazy hornets. Most of the city's students certainly didn't. They gathered in quads and courtyards around the city to watch the spectacle each day, but rarely did one of the onlookers observe the professor fishing notes and diagrams out of a mossy fountain and think, "Now that there's a genius."

The gnomish professor stood only thirty inches high on a good day, or thirty and one half if he wore his fancy shoes, which, unbeknownst to him, he had misplaced several months ago. He had eyeglasses as thick as tea saucers that made his eyes look far too large, and a walrus-like mustache wriggled beneath his shiny red nose. Most days, whenever he arrived wherever it was he was rushing to, his snow-white hair would be standing on end like a cotton ball that spent too long inside a tornado.

He was known to burst into a lecture hall, drop what remained of his belongings in a pile on the desk at the front, and begin furiously scribbling on the chalkboard. About three-quarters of the way through his lesson on mythozoology, magichemistry, or the histories arcane, he would pose a question to the students, flipping around to search for a volunteer with their hand held high in the air.

Sometimes he found another professor sitting in the front row with a bored expression. Other times the hall was totally empty apart from a custodian, who was too busy sweeping beneath the vacant seats to notice Dr. Frazzlefoot had stopped speaking. His magnified eyes would blink a few times, realizing then that he was in the wrong classroom, at the wrong university, on the entirely wrong side of town. The next moment, all in a fluster, he'd sweep up his belongings, hold them tight against his chest, and tear off for the next class.

On the rare occasion that he wound up where he was meant to be, students from across the world gathered to hear him speak. And though many had heard him tell the story of how he developed the arcane generators that now powered the city's many monorails, elevators, escalators, and artificial lights, the tale never lost its luster. He repeated the story not out of some shallow sense of accomplishment or grandeur but merely to encourage the young minds around him—to emphasize how anything is possible, *especially* the impossible.

If he had a silver for every time someone said, "Arcane energy simply isn't sustainable, Fenwick," or, "You're messing with powers you don't understand, Fenwick," or, "By the gods, you're lucky you didn't kill us all man!"— well, let's just say he'd be walking around at thirty-one and a half inches high more often.

The point is that no one ever achieved anything by having a can't-be-done attitude. In fact, most things that are even halfway worth doing will prove somebody else wrong.

The many taverns around Alabaster were always open, and they remained packed with students and educators alike until late into the nights. Fenwick could often be found there in the evenings, sipping tea, telling tales, or leading discussions about complex magical principles that were usually far too advanced for his audience. While he couldn't tell you the name of the place where he stood, or even which side of the city it happened to be on, he *could* discuss at length the interplay between sociological trends and the arcane, as well as magic's many applications for modern technology—and if students gave even the slightest invitation for him to do so, they often found themselves trapped there on the sofa for several hours.

On this night, however, Dr. Frazzlefoot was not in a tavern. He was not sipping tea or conversing with students, and he wasn't sprinting from one place to the next without knowing precisely where he was going. In fact, Fenwick wasn't in Alabaster at all.

The professor was on sabbatical, hundreds of miles away to the south. At the exact moment when the dean of the College of Magicks and Magicianship realized he was no longer in the city, Fenwick was standing in the tropical moonlight of an unnamed island. His hands were raised up to his cheeks, and he was posing a question to a bunch of half-strangers that he never imagined himself asking in the first place.

"Anybody speak frog?"

Just ahead, the island's beach rose into a twisted wall of dark, dense jungle, and two dozen or so slick-skinned, toad-like creatures were spilling from the shadows. Some slipped beneath huge leaves, and others hopped through curtains of vines. Some hung back, whirling slings above their heads in the light of the full moon, while others were croaking and wailing and jamming wooden spears toward the professor's mustache.

"Anybody? Nobody?" Fenwick asked again.

Though he couldn't see the ragtag bunch of hired adventurers behind him, he could hear them humming a *no* through forced smiles. A sort of *nnhnnn* sound.

"Fantastic," the professor said in his happiest, least-threatening tone.

They each took a few careful steps backward, leaning away from the jabbing sticks. Dr. Frazzlefoot was grateful that he'd invested in his new explorer's outfit, which was khaki from head to toe and absolutely covered with pockets. If he'd worn his usual robes, he might have tripped during this little retreat, and, despite his never-ending curiosity, he had absolutely no desire to find out what it felt like to be a kebab. He was especially pleased with his investment in a Pith helmet, which did well to protect his noggin as an errant spear prodded him in the forehead. He backed up a bit quicker after that.

"Back to the boats then, is it?" He asked.

There was a collective grunt of agreement from the others, and they began to ease toward the rowboat, which sat halfway in the sand and halfway in the moon-drenched sea behind them. It might as well have been a mile away. The party smiled and cowered while trying to make themselves look small and uncombative (which wasn't much of a chore for the professor, because he *was* both of those things), but the frogish folk advanced all the same.

Their webbed feet stamped into the sand with a *thwack, thwack, thwack* as half a dozen lunged forward. They thrust their spears, barking in a throaty mix of ribbits and croaks and other sounds one might expect from creatures with big, bulging vocal sacks. The professor certainly didn't understand them, but he nodded along with their hollering.

"No, I absolutely agree," he said. "Trespassing? I think you're quite right. Our mistake. We'll just be going then. Yes. Understood! Why did we come here? A bit of research, it was. No, you're right. We *should* have asked permission."

He carried on like this all the way down the beach, dodging spear tips here and there whenever they grew too close.

"What are they saying?" Mumbled one of the hired hands.

Fenwick thought it might be Rosie. Or was it Rachel?

Runhilda? He wasn't certain he'd even asked their names, but she sure *sounded* like a Rebecca.

"Oh, I haven't the foggiest. Not a clue—none whatsoever. Don't speak frog, you know," Fenwick hummed the words as much as he spoke them. "That said, I do believe when twenty-something spears are aimed at your belly, that's a sort of universal expression for, 'Get on out of here.' Don't you agree?"

By the time they reached the shoreline, the swarm of frog folk had grown to nearly fifty, and small rocks were raining down atop the party's heads like hailstones.

"I told you this hat was a good idea!" Fenwick said as one particularly large pebble plinked off his helmet.

Then, all at once, the slings stopped spinning. The frog folk froze in the sand, and their spears fell to the beach with muffled thuds. The ribbits went quiet, replaced with an eerie hush and the gentle lapping of waves against the shore.

The frogs fell to their knees and began to bow. The shiny skin around their arms glistened in the moonlight as they swayed, up and down and up and down, planting their faces into the sand with each pass. The croaking came back then. It started as a low grumble, slowly swelling into a rhythmic chant that scrambled Fenwick's brain.

"Rana! Rana! Rana! Rana!"

A shadow deepened beside the professor's feet, swallowing the seashells and stretching out along the beach toward the jungle ahead. He turned slowly as if all his joints were rusted and squeaky.

Silently looming over the party, rising from the sea

behind them like a rubbery tidal wave, was a monstrous, vaguely frog-like abomination. Its wart-ridden hide oozed as it stretched over the thing's blubbery form, and half a dozen sticky tentacles, each as wide as a man's torso, wriggled in the spots where arms should have been. Its slack-jawed maw was packed with humungous, human-like teeth, and five bulbous eyes blinked out of sync as it knelt down with a vacant expression. No one moved. Fenwick studied the beast in total fascination, adjusting his glasses to get a better look.

"Well then," he said. "That's a rather big boy, isn't it? What do you suppose it eats? Judging by the blunt teeth, I'd suspect kelp. Or perhaps—"

The creature unleashed a deafening, screechy roar that blew back Fenwick's coattails and at once covered the party in a goopy layer of frog spittle. A cheer of ribbits and croaks erupted from the crowd behind them.

Fenwick wiped a pint of goo from his face, which peeled away in a long stringy mess, then shook it from his hand. The gunk fell to the beach with a splat.

"Rana, everyone. Everyone, Rana."

The professor tried to lift a foot from the puddle of muck beneath him, but the stuff clung to his boot like tacky glue. The next thing he knew, his arms were spinning in a circle, and his rear end went splashing into the goop. As he fell, the leather bag around his shoulder went flying and toppled to the ground, spilling half its contents into the gooey sand.

Through the slime covering his glasses, Fenwick could just make out the cover of a book lying there, and he used his index fingers like little windshield wipers to get a better look.

It was *Essays on Planar Linguistics, Volume Seven.* That one had been especially interesting to write, he recalled, and gathering its research had not been without its fair share of danger, too. All part of the job. Nothing to fear.

The abomination towering above them took a lumbering step forward, and the sand beneath the professor's bottom quaked. As the monster's shadow shifted away from the book, the moonlight revealed something peeking out from behind the volume's cover. Little square corners of parchment. Fenwick plucked the book from the spittle and peeled it open.

They were envelopes, each addressed to the deans of the various colleges which employed him. Inside were letters—the ones announcing his sabbatical.

Fenwick held up one of the sticky envelopes as if he'd made a new discovery and gave it a good smack with the back of his fingers.

"I remember now! *That's* where I left these!"

The creature took another step, its tentacles writhing in time with the chanting of ribbits and croaks.

"Well, this is no good. No good at all," he muttered.

Rana hovered over the professor, its hot breath filling his nose. If he closed his eyes, he might've thought he'd opened a faulty cooler in the fish market on a particularly hot summer day.

It wasn't often that the professor was left puzzled. But as he pinched the letters a bit tighter between his fingers, he just didn't see how he was going to talk his way out of this one.

Dr. Frazzlefoot sighed and looked up to the others. "My new friends, I'm afraid I have some bad news. I'm almost certainly out of a job or two."

JOURNEY'S END

D aybreak always carries with it a bit of magic—
magic that's often found in the quiet moments
when the sun is only just teasing the horizon,
too shy to peek its head above the edge of the world, when
all the sky above and land below is washed in a lavender
glow, not so patiently anticipating those first shimmering
rays that might shake the chill from the night before.

It was just then, in one of these very moments, that
Chamomile returned home for the first time in far, far too
long. She stood resting against the bark of the only resi-
dent of One-Acre Hill, a crooked and wizened oak that sat
squarely in the middle of the mound of grass overlooking

the town. The Grainfields had not changed so very much, she thought, allowing herself this peaceful heartbeat to look about the place with new eyes.

The town was what one might expect of a halfling village. Rolling hills and well-trodden footpaths gently hugged the edges of gardens, babbling streams danced within the emerald valleys, and a few handmade scare-crows with patchwork outfits dotted the lush fields here and there. The sea of tall, golden grass that encircled the place rippled like waves in the breeze, all shimmering and painted gray in the last traces of full moonlight.

It was springtime now, and the gardens were nearly ripe; some swollen with vegetables fit for canning, others with fruits for pies (a bushel or two of which would be baked this very morning, no doubt). There was ivy, too, much of which had dared to climb the nearby picket fences to crawl up windows and around chimneys, searching for those spaces where the light shone just right in the heat of the day.

Chamomile stood in the still of it all, the pre-dawn chill biting at the tips of her fingers and the edges of her ears. The Grainfields seemed so very small, smaller now than ever before, and quiet beyond measure, except of course for the robins and finches who were busy rehearsing for their morning chorus. All across town, the windows were dark and the chimneys free of smoke, but from her perch above it all, she could still make out the first signs of life emerging into the world.

On the eastern side of town, lazily hobbling his way up a winding dirt path, was Poplin Tinkertot, a flickering lantern shaking in his outstretched hand. Though it wasn't much brighter than a star from where she stood, Chamomile recognized his stooped posture and the shadow of a satchel full of mail bouncing against his hip. Toward the west, Cecilia Brandylane was standing outside the dusty green doors to The Gilded Gopher, fumbling with a ring of too many keys.

"Breakfast won't cook itself," she used to say, and she was likely reciting the very same now, many mornings after Chamomile first heard her speak the phrase.

The chickens outside Mr. Baldbelly's were just beginning to stir, preening and pecking about, stretching their necks in the way that chickens often do before announcing the arrival of first light. Mr. Baldbelly himself had even braved his way into the cool of the morning to spread a bit of feed along the grass. There were others too, some lighting lanterns behind misty windows or stepping onto dewy porches to sip tea and coffee with the sunrise. A stirring had begun, soft and gentle, but signaling the start of the busy yet not-so-busy day to come.

It all seemed so familiar, but not without the little changes that years often bring. There were one or two new homes in places where empty hills once stood, a new garden outside the Burrows' residence, and several freshly painted fences running in places where fences hadn't been before. There were familiar sights, too, and these far outweighed the new ones. The tavern still stood where it always had, sun-beaten and rarely empty, and several barns sat rocking on their foundations, patiently awaiting the repairs they'd been requesting since before Chamomile departed. The streams still whispered in their secret language, the trees still offered rooms within their roots for napping, and the many homes throughout the fields, quiet and shadowy as they were, still greeted Chamomile as an old friend, as they always had and always would.

The Grainfields had not changed so very much, after all, but Chamomile had. She'd traveled to the ends of the world, beyond even, and was no longer the young girl she'd been when taking those brave first steps into the wild. She now knew friendship, and loss, and pain, and triumph, and wonder, and what it meant to stand when others could not or would not.

Her journey was over, or was soon to be, but its traces still lingered in her bones. The scars along her arms and legs were only just beginning to heal, and though a few had turned to silver with time, the wounds beneath burned like new whenever she traced her fingers overtop them or glimpsed their shape in her reflection. She hadn't forgotten how she earned them, not one.

Returning here, to The Grainfields, to normal, seemed a quest far beyond the trials of the last few years. To wind down in the tavern at the end of the day, to speak of the weather, to meekly request a cup of flour from a neighbor, to lazily wonder what the day might bring—mundane though these acts might be—seemed altogether foreign to her now. Even to stand where she stood, patiently awaiting the arrival of the sun without glancing over her shoulder for something unseen, felt strangely new and unfamiliar.

When the day began, and when Chamomile's neighbors found that her windows were now open and the ivy across her door had been carefully plucked free, they would welcome her home with song and dance and too much hugging. They would bring her sweets and bread and tea and beg to hear her tale—to know what it had been like to brave the waters of an angry sea, to climb fierce mountains, to delve into the darkest reaches of the world. They would ask with eyes wide, shimmering with wonder, knees bobbing in anticipation of the story she'd weave.

But did she even know the words? There was so much to tell—too much—and she feared she could not find them. How does one begin to capture the swelling sound of a dragon's throat or the heat of the flames that follow shortly after? Could she ever really convey the sting of a great serpent's bite or the emptiness that settles into one's chest as a dear friend breathes his last? How could she describe that hurt beyond hurt that seeps into every muscle and bone long after one's legs have turned to jelly yet still march on and on and on? Would her words do justice to the nights spent sleeping beneath thin wool sheets along a cliff's edge or tossing and turning in the heat of a volcano's belly? Could she really describe hunger? Would she manage to find the phrase to capture the bittersweet melancholy of having succeeded in a quest but at a cost too great to ever repay?

It was during these questions, the ones without answers, that Chamomile slid her chilled-through hands into her pockets in search of warmth. With a bit of a sting, she stumbled across something she didn't expect. Her fingertips caressed the tip of a pen, one given to her long ago and far away by a friend who could no longer cherish the words it might write. She traced the worn wood of its body, rolling it over between her fingers as she peered at the horizon, where the first sliver of light had just broken free.

Perhaps she could write it down—all of it. Maybe, with time, the right words could be found, and she could capture them between ink and paper. Is that what they would have wanted? Is that what *she* wanted?

The light of day blossomed over the hills, washing over Chamomile and bathing The Grainfields below in the dim, golden glow of a new day. She closed her eyes, letting the warm rays soak into her rosy cheeks as the sounds of morning spread throughout the town. She brushed the pen a final time, lifted her pack from the ground, and set out toward the small yellow door in the distance. When she arrived, she would place the pen along the mantle above her hearth, a space reserved only for those trinkets which deserved to be seen each day. There it would stay, free from the labor of writing until her time in The Grainfields came to a close.

When asked about the quest, she would speak long and fondly of those moments worth sharing: The impossible sights. The thrilling battles. The daring escapes. The countless treasures. The cries of victory. The days of celebration.

She would spend every precious evening in The Gilded Gopher, spinning tales of her days beyond The Grainfields, recalling dream-like memories to anyone who felt compelled to listen, giving each neighbor some little sense of adventure and doing so freely.

But, even years from now, once every story had been told a dozen times, only Chamomile would know all there was to know. Because there were other memories, too, ones that were not so simple to explain, ones for which words could only do so much justice. And those memories —those bits in between—would remain hers and hers alone, as they already were.

She knew now that putting pen to paper would be a journey for which there is no end, that no number of days or drafts could ever truly capture it. Not really, anyway.

After all, adventures are meant to be lived, but a tale is only as good as its telling.

ACKNOWLEDGMENTS

I would be a fool not to begin by first thanking my wife, Brooke. Despite telling me at least two-dozen times that you preferred to read things yourself (rather than hear them read aloud), you always listened. I hope the funny voices made it a bit more enjoyable. Your patience is limitless.

To my parents and the many friends and family members who encouraged me along the way: You are the world's greatest cheerleaders, and I couldn't have done this without you. I finally published something, Dad. Are you happy now?

I am endlessly grateful to Adam and Eric for the years of friendship and countless adventures, both real and imagined. Thank you for showing me new worlds and spending your days in this one alongside me.

I must also extend my gratitude to Dr. Teresa Jones, who upon reading one of my stories in college said, "I can't help you if you don't want to be helped," and at once made me cry and a better writer.

Thank you to my editor, Katie Lasitter, for your sharp eyes and lack of filter. These stories were made better because of you. And, of course, my thanks to Bodie H. for bringing these tales to life with your whimsical art.

To my living room adventuring party, Kat, Alex, and Brooke, thank you for sharing a story with me and inspiring so many others. One day, when that tale has finally been told, I'll continue to carry it with me forever.

A very special thank you to the many kind folks in the tabletop gaming, miniature painting, and crafting communities who welcomed me with open arms and read many of my first drafts. This book exists, in no small part, thanks to your endless kindness and support.

Lastly, thank you to Finn. You contributed absolutely nothing to the writing process, and your feedback was mostly incomprehensible, but you were and are and will always be an endless source of inspiration. Thank you for that.

I hope you read this one day. I hope these little stories inspire you to set out on your own adventures. I hope I can tag along on a few of them. But more than anything, I hope you know that you are loved, and that you're never too old to play pretend.

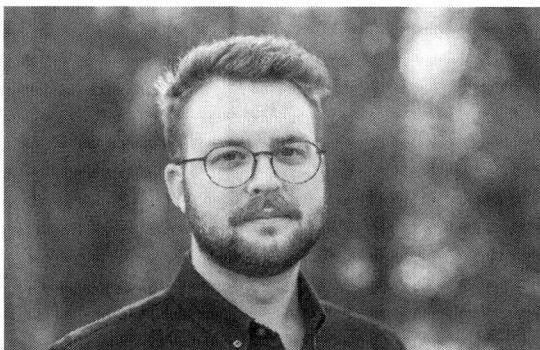

J. E. TANKERSLEY was raised in a single-gas-station town in South Carolina where there was little else to do but create worlds of his own. What began with weaving plots for action figures and swinging sticks for swords in the backyard grew into a love of fantasy and storytelling that never left. Today, he lives and writes in a town with many gas stations along with his wife and son. When he isn't writing, you can usually find him around the tabletop, rolling dice, exploring imaginary worlds, and making memories as real as any others.

For more book updates and general nerdiness, follow me on Instagram.

instagram.com/modestmimic

Printed in Poland
by Amazon Fulfillment
Poland Sp. z o.o., Wrocław

86013107R00127